Drina Dances Again

**Previous books in the
Drina series:**

Drina Dances Again

Jean Estoril

Illustrated by Jenny Sanders

AN
APPLE
PAPERBACK

SCHOLASTIC INC.
New York Toronto London Auckland Sydney

The illustrator would like to acknowledge the help of
Cathy Marston, the young dancer,
and her teacher, Maureen Mitchell,
of the Eden Dance Centre in Cambridge.

ISBN 0-590-42557-9

12 11 10 9 8 7 6 5 4 3 2   0 1 2 3/9

Printed in the U.S.A.   11

First Scholastic printing, October 1989

A Note to Readers

Drina Dances Again is set in England. A few of the British places and terms you may not be familiar with are listed below.

Covent Garden — London's opera house, and the home of the Royal Ballet.
the Strand — a street in the main theater district of London.
Tattoo — a form of entertainment consisting of outdoor military exercises done to music.
the Tube — the London subway.
the West End — London's theater district.

Here are some ballet terms you may not know:

barre — a bar attached to the wall which dancers use to maintain their balance.

corps de ballet — literally means "the body of the ballet"; chorus or the ensemble dancers.

divertissement — solo pieces within a ballet, which usually have nothing to do with the story of the ballet.

pas de deux — literally means "a step for two."

prima ballerina assoluta — literally means "absolutely first ballerina"; the highest title of praise for a ballerina.

CONTENTS

BOOK ONE

Summer Term at the Dominick

1

Beginning of Term

Drina was sitting on a seat in Lincoln's Inn Fields. It was half-past eight on the first Tuesday in May and soon she must hurry on to the Dominick Ballet School in Red Lion Square. It would never do to be late on the first day of term, and, contrary to the usual custom, Easter had been so late that ballet classes and school lessons were to start on the same morning.

It was a glorious day, already hot, and the sunshine had woken her early, which accounted for the fact that she had left the flat in Westminster a quarter of an hour before her usual time and so was able to linger under the brilliant green of the trees in one of London's largest squares. In the distance she could hear the traffic roaring along Kingsway and in the square itself cars were continually arriving, bringing people to work. But, alone on her seat, Drina felt a little removed from the noise and bustle of London and it was good to have a breathing space, however slight.

It was only a very few days since she had returned from Italy and there hadn't been much time for thinking. Only a week before she had been in Genoa, and she wrinkled up her brow, remembering. On Tuesday last week she and Antonia had gone shopping in the Via XX Settembre, and then had wandered by the Port and visited the rather desolate Palazzo Doria, once so great and splendid, but badly bombed in the war and now only a shadow of its former self. Drina had loved Genoa, and she had thoroughly enjoyed the company of her Italian cousin. She very much hoped that Antonia, only a year older than herself, would be able to visit London soon. It still seemed strange that she had got to know her Italian relations at last: her father's mother in Milan and the Gardinos in Genoa. There were other cousins further South and she would almost certainly return to Italy and visit them.

But seeing new places and meeting new people had not been the biggest thrill of those weeks in Italy. Less than a week ago, on the Wednesday, Drina and Emilia Riante – an Italian student from Chalk Green, the Dominick residential school in Buckinghamshire – had had the wonderful experience of dancing with the Dominick Company. It had been pure chance, because some of the youngest members of the *corps de ballet* had been ill after eating lobster. To dance with the Dominick when she was only fourteen! Every time Drina remembered that night her heart leaped and she was filled with incredulity. Already it seemed a fantastic dream, and now the usual hard work lay in front of her, with no more extraordinary and unlikely experiences.

There certainly might have been one more exciting experience in the near future, but Drina had written a letter on Sunday evening that had put an end to that possibility. She had returned home to find a letter waiting for her from Calum Campbell, the man who had produced the play *Argument in Paris* in which Drina had once acted in the West End. He suggested that she should be auditioned for the part of Margaret in Barrie's *Dear Brutus* and, since this was one of Drina's favourite plays, she had been very tempted. But clearly her dancing came first and so she had decided to turn her back on the straight theatre. All the same, it would have been wonderful to play the "might-have-been" girl who was left in the magic wood.

"But I couldn't!" Drina said aloud to a friendly sparrow. "I *had* to turn it down. I really must work this term." Since she always worked hard there was not the slightest need to lecture herself, but what she really meant was that she must cut out all distractions, anything that would take her mind off her ballet training.

Sitting there, Drina's mind began to wander towards her return to the Dominick. It was a pity that her friend Rose Conway was still at Chalk Green, and likely to be for another two or three terms, but there was always Ilonka, the Lynzonian girl with whom she had grown so friendly the previous term. Ilonka would be happy now, for her father had at last managed to escape from behind the Iron Curtain. Drina was deeply glad about that. There was Igor Dominick, too, the great Igor Dominick's only son. But would he still be friendly when they were both back at the Dominick School? Last term, his first, he had made himself very unpopular, because he so clearly preferred his Paris ballet school and because he had rather an odd, supercilious manner. But in Milan, during the first week of the Company's tour, he and Drina had grown rather friendly and, meeting again in Genoa, had continued to get to know each other.

Could she, however, tell with Igor? He was older and in the class above her. Maybe they would be back where they started, and Drina knew that she would be sorry. Still, there would be nothing that she could do about it.

It was twenty to nine. She leaped up, seized her case

and, crossing the square, returned to Kingsway. A few moments later she spied Ilonka hurrying towards her. She was waving a newspaper and looked excited, but then Ilonka was easily moved to happiness, excitement or despair.

"Oh, Drina! I thought I would come to meet you, knowing that you usually walk up here."

"I'm glad you did," Drina said cheerfully. "Though you might easily have missed me. I've been sitting in Lincoln's Inn Fields."

"But I was so pleased to see your picture – so excited. Last night I nearly telephoned."

"What picture?" Drina asked blankly, staring at the paper being waved under her nose. It was the previous day's London *Evening Standard*.

"You mean you haven't seen? You do not know?"

"I haven't the faintest idea what you're talking about, Ilonka."

Ilonka drew her out of the stream of hurrying people and indicated a large photograph on an inner page.

"There! It is so pretty!"

Drina literally gaped at the photograph. It was of a girl doing a graceful arabesque by a fountain, with cypresses and statues in the background. The caption read: *"This charming picture was sent to us by one of our readers and he calls it 'Young Girl by a Fountain'. The attractive young dancer is Miss Drina Adams, a pupil at the Dominick Ballet School in London. She will be remembered as the girl who took the part of Françoise in the play* Argument *in Paris."*

"Good heavens!" Drina said frankly.

"You really did not know?"

"I really didn't. Igor must have sent it in. He did threaten to send it to a ballet magazine if it was good, but I thought he was teasing."

"But where –?"

"On Isola Bella in Lake Maggiore. I didn't know that anyone was watching and it was so lovely I *had* to dance."

"Terza says it is very nice publicity."

"I suppose it is," Drina said doubtfully, wondering what her grandmother would have to say about it. Mrs Chester, who had brought her up since the death of her mother when Drina was only a baby, was a rather stiff sort of person and not at all fond of publicity. However, it did seem to show that Igor was still aware of her existence and Drina was somehow glad of that.

"You may have this. You would like to keep it?"

"Oh, thank you very much. We only take *The Times*." Drina folded the paper and put it in her case. They walked on together, soon overtaking Daphne Daniety, whom Drina had known for many years, since her Willerbury days.

"She *is* getting most dreadfully tall," Drina breathed, as they approached Daphne, who was walking slowly.

"Yes. She has grown, I think, since last term."

Daphne looked at them without enthusiasm. She was intensely jealous of Drina and never very friendly.

"Ah, here's the little Drina! I saw your photograph. I suppose you sent it in yourself?"

Drina flushed. She was always sorry that Daphne disliked her so much.

"I didn't, you know. I hadn't even seen it until Ilonka showed me a few minutes ago. It was Igor."

"*Igor!*" Daphne looked astounded, as well she might. Igor Dominick had not shown the slightest friendliness to any of them during the previous term.

"Yes. He was in Italy with the Company and I was there visiting relations. I was dancing and didn't even know he was there, taking a photograph."

"A likely story!" said Daphne, with a sniff. She sounded like a character in a bad novel.

"It's true, all the same," Drina said mildly, thinking that Daphne certainly didn't look as though she had just had over three weeks' holiday. She was very pale and her mousy hair, once so fair, looked limp and dull. To add to her plainness she had a spot on her chin.

"And I will tell you something else that is true," said Ilonka, walking on Drina's other side. "In Genoa, Drina danced with the Dominick Company."

"Oh, I believe *that*," Daphne said, with heavy sarcasm, at the same moment as Drina murmured, "*Do shut up, Ilonka!*"

"But it is true. Drina and Emilia."

"I suppose you mean they walked on or something? Pushed themselves forward just because they were there when the Company was."

Ilonka was beginning to look thoroughly indignant. She was fond of Drina, who had been very kind to her when she was unhappy and strange to England.

"It wasn't like that. Some members of the *corps de ballet* were ill and so Drina and Emilia danced. They were two of the May Queen's attendants in *The Lonely Princess*."

"It was only for one night," said Drina quietly, and she was glad when they reached Red Lion Square and Daphne went off to join Queenie, Betty and Jill, who were waving from the steps of the Dominick School.

"I wish you hadn't told her," she said, when Daphne was out of earshot. Ilonka snorted.

"And why not? That one I do not like. She always thinks one is telling lies."

"She isn't very nice, but I don't want to make her dislike me any more."

But it seemed that Daphne would not, in any case,

have been able to avoid hearing about Drina's experience in Genoa, because the moment Drina entered the cloakroom it was clear that the news had got out. She was immediately surrounded by an interested little crowd, all wanting to know what it had felt like to dance with the Dominick. Most people were envious, but not bitterly jealous, like Daphne.

"But who told you?" Drina asked, hastily taking off the red dress that was the summer uniform, and struggling into her practice clothes.

"I don't know where it came from in the first place," said Meryl. "One of the boys, I think. Didn't young Igor Dominick dance, too?"

"And then there was your photograph in the paper yesterday," said Bella Giornio, an Italian girl who had been at the Dominick for some years.

"*Clearly* sent there by Drina herself," said Queenie Rothington, who was even more jealous of Drina than Daphne.

Drina disdained to answer, but Ilonka said shrilly, "It was Igor. Drina didn't know."

"Why *should* Igor?" Queenie asked nastily. "He doesn't even know that Drina exists."

"They became friendly in Italy. They were on Isola Bella together."

Altogether Drina was quite glad to leave the cloakroom and start making her way towards the studios. Fame, even such mild fame, was all very well, but it always seemed to bring unpleasantness in its train. She saw Igor Dominick lounging at a corner ahead and her heart leaped. Italy had given him a deep tan and he looked even more handsome than she remembered. Also, with that casual, lounging attitude, just about as unapproachable as he had done last term.

But he grinned when he saw her and said cheerfully,

"Hullo, Drina! Back then to the old grind?"

"Yes," agreed Drina. "Doesn't Italy seem far away?"

"In another life." He fell into step with her and Ilonka and talked in a friendly way until they were forced to separate, Igor going on to the next studio for his ballet class. Drina was conscious of a warm happiness. So he really was going to be different! It was a relief, partly because she did like him very much and partly because she knew that, in his heart, he had hated being friendless and unpopular last term.

She looked round the big, light studio with pleasure. It was good to be back at the Dominick; good to know that a busy term lay ahead. And then there was no more time for anything but dancing, for the ballet teacher appeared and the class started. Later, in the classroom overlooking Red Lion Square, they copied out timetables and were given new books, and by lunch-time Italy was more than ever a dream.

When Drina was ready to leave the Dominick at four o'clock that afternoon, she found Rose waiting in the hall, close to the glass case that held Elizabeth Ivory's ballet shoes. Elizabeth Ivory, the great dancer, had been Drina's mother, but, though Rose knew, very few other people did. It was Drina's closely guarded secret and she intended it to remain so.

Rose wore her Chalk Green uniform dress – a bright emerald instead of scarlet – and looked even paler than Daphne. Rose lived in a small, overcrowded house at Earls Court and had missed the air of the Chiltern Hills. But Drina thought with a sudden feeling of pleasure that Rose was growing very pretty. She would never be very striking perhaps – her colouring was too pale – but her brown hair was curlier than it used to be and her skin was very clear.

Rose was talking to Jan Williams, a boy whom she

and Drina liked very much, but she spun round when Drina approached.

"Hullo, Drina! I saw your photograph. I thought it was simply lovely and Mum was quite thrilled."

"Daphne and Queenie hate me for it," Drina said gloomily. "But Igor said at lunch-time that he really does mean to send it to a ballet magazine. I've said he can, but–"

"Well, who cares what Queenie and Daphne think?" said Rose boldly, though she did care, never having been at ease with either of them.

As they turned to leave, Marianne Volonaise, Director of the School and the Company, came through the front door.

"Congratulations on the photograph, Drina," she said, smiling. "You look charming and it might have been taken by a professional. It was very clever of Igor. He says it was on Isola Bella."

"Yes, Madam," said Drina. "The day he came out with us."

"And now you're ready for more hard work?"

"Oh, yes!"

"I hear you've decided not to try for the part in *Dear Brutus*?"

"Yes-s. It was tempting, but I thought – thought I ought to concentrate on my dancing."

"Perhaps you're wise, though it would only have been for a short time. Two weeks I believe it's to run." And Miss Volonaise nodded in a friendly way and passed on.

"I don't know how you can talk to her as though she were an ordinary human being," said Rose, as the two went out into the square alone.

"Well, I suppose she is," said Drina, a trifle defensively. There had been a time when she was deeply in awe of Marianne Volonaise, but now she seemed to know her quite well.

"Not to me. Nor to most people. I can never forget that she holds our fates in her hands."

"I know," Drina agreed. "To some extent, anyway. I suppose we partly hold our own, if you know what I mean."

"Well, we can work hard, but so many things might affect us. Sometimes I feel quite helpless, thinking of all the things that *could* happen."

In the square the sun was very hot and they idled along. Drina was suddenly startled to hear a boy's voice calling her name. She swung round and saw a dark-haired boy who was not wearing the Dominick uniform.

"Why, *Mark*!"

She had known Mark Playford in her Willerbury days and they had gone to the Selswick Dancing School together. Mark was a little older than her, almost exactly the same age as Jenny Pilgrim, who would be fifteen next month.

He was smiling cheerfully.

"I thought you'd be surprised."

"Surprised! I'm amazed. What are you doing here? Oh, Rose, this is Mark Playford from Willerbury. He's a friend of Jenny's. Rose goes to the residential school at Chalk Green, Mark."

Mark and Rose nodded and said, "How do you do?" and then Mark went on:

"I've been here since one o'clock. They've been auditioning all day in the rehearsal rooms."

"Oh! I did hear a good while ago that you might try for the Dominick, but Jenny didn't tell me when she last wrote –"

"I don't think she knew. I haven't seen her for a

while. Hasn't she been away at her precious farm? Anyway, I've been accepted as a full-time student for next September. Mum was with me, but she went off to do some shopping. They asked me to stay behind for a few minutes."

"Oh, I'm so glad!" And Drina meant it sincerely. She had always liked Mark. "Congratulations!"

He grinned.

"I'm pleased, but I do wonder what it will be like. A great change from my Willerbury school, that's clear. I'm not used to girls. You'll have to hold my hand!"

"I'll introduce you to people," Drina said willingly. "And you don't have ballet classes with the girls. You'll know Daphne as well, of course."

"Yes," he agreed, without any marked enthusiasm. "Anyway, I may see you again before September. Will you be visiting the Pilgrims in Willerbury?"

"Well, in the summer holidays, perhaps. Jenny and I hope to go to the farm. I was going at Easter, but then I went to Italy instead."

They parted in Kingsway, Mark disappearing into the tube station, and Drina and Rose walked on rapidly.

"He looks nice," Rose said. "Nicer than Igor Dominick. More ordinary and friendly."

"He *is* nice," Drina agreed. "But Igor is so interesting and funny. I'm really glad Mark's coming to the Dominick in September. Funny how we three Willerbury ones have got here! And Miss Selswick, too." For Janetta Selswick was now attached to the Dominick School, having given up her own school some time before.

In the Strand they caught a bus that would take them to Parliament Square, for Rose was going to have tea with Drina. Though it was only a short journey they went on top and sat by an open window with their hair blowing in the hot wind.

"It seems to have been a long day," Drina said thoughtfully. "But I enjoyed most of it. Oh, Rose, I do wish you were at the Dominick!"

"I shall be again next year," Rose remarked. "In a way I shall be glad, but I love Chalk Green. It will be lovely to get back there and draw breaths of real country air. I wonder if the hawthorn will be out?"

"Not yet, surely? It's generally nearer the middle of May. London *is* hot!" And they sat in companionable silence while the bus swept down Whitehall, then rose and hurried down the stairs. The scene was so familiar that Drina scarcely noticed it, but when Big Ben struck a quarter to five she glanced up.

"I must have been late leaving the Dominick. I do want my tea! I'm starving and dying of thirst."

They hurried past St Margaret's and were soon in the entrance hall of the block of flats where Drina lived with her grandparents. And Drina was happily conscious that at least she and Rose would have the evening together. She always missed her friend when she went back to Chalk Green.

2

Drina at Chalk Green

For several days life went on peacefully enough at the Dominick School and Drina felt that she was well into the rhythm of the term. With Ilonka, Meryl, Bella and some of the other girls she was content, and there were also Jan Williams and Igor Dominick. Igor was certainly a reformed character and seemed to be making friends. He was no longer so remote and supercilious and he often looked for Drina in the canteen.

Ilonka was very happy, for her father was safely with them and, though not yet in very good health, he was delighted to be in England after his terrible experiences behind the Iron Curtain that it seemed he would soon be much better.

"We are to buy a restaurant," Ilonka explained, when she met Drina one morning. "Terza is to lend the money. She is making so very much with her book." Ilonka's sister had written a best-selling book called *Diary of a Dancer*.

"What will you call it?"

"Well, at first we thought 'The Blue Danube', but that is too – too ordinary. There might perhaps be another with that name. So now we think perhaps 'The Golden Zither', with a sign painted by an artist my father knows."

"Oh, I like that! It's a musical instrument, isn't it?"

And Drina was very thrilled with her friends' plans.

The hot weather had given place to cooler air and showers, but the London parks were beautiful with flowering trees, and the azaleas were almost out by the lake in St James's Park.

"*I do love London in May,*" Drina wrote to Jenny, in Willerbury. "*The trees are so vividly green and the blossom is beautiful. Yesterday we went to Kew and the lilac was out. Oh, Jenny, it seems so long since I saw you. Italy was wonderful – I wouldn't have missed it – but I would like to see you, and the farm, and my dear cat, Esmeralda.*"

On Monday there was a letter from Rose that made Drina wrinkle up her brows worriedly.

"*Dear Drina,*

"*Well, I got back here on Wednesday and at first, in the train, everything was fun and it was glorious to see the country again, with the hawthorn in bud, the cow parsley coming out and the early buttercups. But the most awful thing has happened. Hildegarde isn't coming back. Her mother has been ill and apparently she'll never be very well again. They want Hildegarde to be nearer, so she is going to a ballet school in Freiburg and living at home. That would be bad enough, because I liked Hildegarde very much, but of course it meant that there was an empty bed in our bedroom at Ivory, and the first thing we saw when we went upstairs was Christine Gifford sitting on it, doing her nails. Apparently she had got to know about Hildegarde in the holidays and had written to Matron, telling her that she would sooner be in Ivory than Markova, and Matron did what she was asked.*

"*It gives the girls in Markova a breathing space – as you know, she didn't get on well with them and there were often ructions – but nothing worse could possibly have happened to me. I've never liked her, and I'm really almost afraid of her,* she has such critical eyes and says such horrible things, like Queenie and Daphne, though almost worse than either. The twins don't take much notice of her. You know how absorbed in each other Joan and Sue are? And Emilia puts up with her, though she doesn't like her. Bianca is plain scared of her, but it's me who gets the brunt of it. She has the bed next to mine and she keeps on saying such terrible things and raising her eyebrows at my belongings.

"I've tried very hard not to mind being poor, when most of the others are quite well off or even downright rich, and of course my uniform is all right, because I get a grant for that. But there are such a lot of other things. I haven't got a writing-case or a portable radio and my dressing-gown is faded and much too short, and all the others have the loveliest underclothes. Christine has got the most beautiful things that she bought in Paris, and her pyjamas are pink with lace on, and blue with little roses. Mine are old and faded and every time I put them on she looks at me in that awful way of hers. But I shouldn't mind if it were only looks, but she never loses an opportunity to say something crushing about my not having a proper holiday and asking where I live and what my father does. When I said he was a plumber she actually laughed. I nearly smacked her face and that would have shown her that I'm no lady! Her father is something in the Foreign Office. Sue has told her to shut up several times, but it doesn't do any good and if things go on like this I shall run away or something."

Drina was very angry and upset when she had finished Rose's letter. Snobbery was much disliked at the Dominick School in London, where the pupils were from homes of every sort, some poor and some rich, and it was certainly not encouraged at Chalk Green. If the headmistress, Miss Sutherland, knew of Christine's behaviour there would probably be trouble, but unless

Rose complained . . . .

Drina worried all day and that evening asked permission to telephone her friend. Rose was fetched to the phone and she certainly didn't sound her usual cheerful self.

"Oh, Drina, how nice to hear your voice! How I wish you were here!"

"Aren't things any better with Christine?"

"Better? No, worse. I expect I shouldn't let her get under my skin, but I can scarcely bear to be in the same room with her. And she *knows* how I feel and that makes her worse. A sense of power, I suppose."

"Look, Rose! I'll try and come up. I hate you to be miserable. You ought to tell Matron or someone."

"I couldn't, though one of the twins threatened to do it."

"You *must*. I'll come and see you. I'll ask Grandfather if he could drive me out there on Saturday."

But when she went back into the sitting-room Mr Chester shook his head.

"I would have done, my dear, but I'm going to meet the Australian manager on Saturday."

"What is all this?" Mrs Chester asked, looking up from her sewing.

"Rose is miserable and I want to see her."

"Well, you can't bear *her* troubles."

"No, but I may be able to talk sense into her. It's that wretched Christine. She's bullying Rose. Couldn't I go by myself? I could get the train to Saunderton and then walk. It isn't very far. Rose might be able to meet me and we could have a picnic lunch. They're very free at Chalk Green on Saturdays and I expect Miss Sutherland would let her."

Mrs Chester looked doubtfully at her granddaughter. Drina was rapidly growing very independent and there was really no reason why she should not travel to Buckinghamshire alone.

"Oh, I suppose so, if you really want to go. A day in the country will do you good. You seem to be working very hard. But I don't see why you should tackle Rose's problems."

"Because she's my friend," said Drina quietly and, when her school work was finished, she looked up a train and then wrote a note to Rose, telling her that she hoped to arrive at Saunderton soon after twelve-thirty and that she would bring a picnic lunch for both of them.

Saturday was a perfect day, warm and golden, and Drina was in high spirits as she sat in the train at Marylebone. It would be lovely to see everyone at Chalk Green and immensely satisfying to see her beloved Chilterns. The brilliant, exotic beauty of Italy had appealed to her strongly, but during those months at Chalk Green the gentle, muted beauty of the hills had really penetrated her heart, and she loved them in all seasons and all weathers.

She read peacefully until London was left behind and the fields and trees began. At her first sight of a beech wood, so sharply green under the brilliant sky, she put the book away and stood by the open window with her hair blowing. The hawthorn was out in places and the fields were golden with buttercups.

High Wycombe, with the houses and factories climbing the hills on either side of the deep valley and then fields again. West Wycombe church, the satisfying curves of the ridges, the russet-roofed, flint-walled farms that always looked as though they had grown out of that pale, flinty earth. In the valley near Bradenham the buttercups made carpets of continuous

yellow and the cow parsley frothed and foamed under the hawthorn hedges.

Rose, in her emerald green dress, was standing on the little platform at Saunderton, holding Petrouchka on a lead. Drina hurried towards them, rapturously sniffing the sweet air and enjoying the sun on her bare head. Petrouchka began to bark wildly and to caper about on the end of the lead. Drina had rescued him once when he was hurt, so he had always regarded Drina as his one and only mistress, even though he had nearly ninety other devoted friends at Chalk Green.

Drina snatched him up and kissed his black and white head.

"Well, my angel! You never forget me, do you? Hullo, Rose!"

"Oh, Drina, I *am* glad to see you!"

"So am I to see you. And isn't this wonderful?" Drina cried, hitching the little rucksack that held their lunch.

They soon turned up the lane that led to the footpath up Lodge Hill and, by mutual consent, the subject of Christine was not mentioned. It could wait until they were settled high on the flat-topped hill they both loved. So they circled a field full of cows, climbed a couple of stiles where the nettles were already vicious, and were soon climbing up the smooth turf of the hill, with the Chiltern scene spread out behind and below them – Princes Risborough across the valley and the great white chalk splash of Whiteleaf Cross on the side of the opposite hills, the long sweeps of the brilliant beech woods, and a train travelling towards the Vale and distant Banbury.

As they climbed, Drina told about the happenings at the Dominick, and when they flung themselves down in their favourite place on the hill's edge, looking over the little bushes of dogwood and wild privet to Bledlow

Ridge, Drina unpacked the food and gave Rose her share.

"And there's iced lemonade, because I knew we'd be thirsty. Now, Rose, is it really as bad as you said in your letter?"

"It's worse," Rose said gloomily. "But I'm sorry I moaned so dreadfully. I *hate* Christine! She's getting worse instead of better. She's fifteen in July and will be going to the Dominick in September, I believe –"

"Oh, heaven help me! Queenie and Daphne *and* Christine!"

"But you won't have to share a bedroom with them and, even if you did, you have the loveliest things and they couldn't possibly be snobbish about you."

"They ought not to be snobbish about anyone. And I'm sure your father is as nice and as good-looking and all the rest as Christine's."

"He's nicer," Rose said warmly. "A million times nicer. Mr Gifford is fat and pompous-looking."

"I'm not surprised. I can't imagine Christine with *pleasant* parents. After all, she must have got her horridness from somewhere. But look here, Rose! You'll have to do *something*. It may only be for a term – "

"A term feels like a lifetime to me. But I really can't, Drina. Think what Christine would say then."

"She couldn't be worse than she is, and the others would all sympathize with you. I don't believe in rushing to the staff and telling tales, but this time I think it would be fully justified. Tell Miss Sutherland. She's understanding and will see that Christine is removed quietly from your dormitory, I'm sure she will."

"*You* didn't when you shared with Christine."

Drina looked thoughtful.

"I was new, and I soon learned to manage her, though I never liked her. I was heartily glad when you came and she was moved into Markova."

"I shall *never* learn to manage her. I'm not like you. I haven't got a temper and – and a presence."

Drina looked at the pretty, rather gentle face of her friend.

"I said I'd kill her if she touched my things again, and I almost meant it. She was poking about in my private writing-case. But I see that you can't cope with her. You really will have to do something, and soon. Go to Miss Sutherland this evening after tea. Promise?"

Rose buried her nose in the warm turf, where, soon, the purple thyme would be so fragrant.

"All right. Perhaps I will. Only – "

"*Promise.*"

"Very well, and I'm sorry to be so feeble. And now I feel better, though I do dread what will happen."

"Nothing much will happen, except that Christine may get a telling-off that will make her realize what a beast she is. Now let's go to the Manor and then perhaps up on Bledlow Cross."

They picked up all their papers and every scrap of orange peel, since both had a horror of leaving litter in a beautiful place. Then, calling Petrouchka, they pushed their way down on to the broad path on the other side of the hill. Twenty minutes later they were approaching the tiny hamlet of Chalk Green, where Drina insisted on going into the little village shop and post office to see her old friend and buy sweets.

"It's so sleepy; so quiet!" she said, looking affectionately at the half-dozen little flint cottages. "It always astonishes me to remember that London is so near."

At the Manor dinner was over and the students were ready to enjoy their various Saturday pursuits: a few to go riding, others cycling, and yet more to walk over the hills.

Miss Crawford was washing down her car in the stable-yard and greeted Drina with pleasure.

"Hello, my dear! How nice to see you! And how's the Dominick?"

"It's splendid," Drina assured her. "And I'm working really hard."

"You always do, I know. I suppose Petrouchka was pleased to see you?"

"He nearly murdered me! He still thinks he's *my* dog."

"That's because you found him when he was in trouble. Are you all going for a walk?"

"Through the woods and on to Bledlow Cross," Drina said.

They were joined by Emilia and her little sister Bianca and set off happily. Now that she had made up her mind what to do, Rose was in good spirits, and not even a meeting with Christine, mounted on her chestnut mare, damped her. Christine merely looked down her nose, ignoring them.

"Beast!" said Emilia.

"I hate her!" said little Bianca, who had enjoyed her first term at Chalk Green and who was finding the presence of Christine in Ivory a very poor exchange for good-tempered, friendly Hildegarde.

The woods were already so thick that the sunlight scarcely came through and they walked in a green gloom, their feet swishing through the dry leaves of other years.

High on the hill's edge they pushed through the thick masses of wild privet until they stood on the turf above the Vale, with little white Bledlow Cross at their feet. In one place the turf had been cut and Drina fell on her knees to stare indignantly at the huge initials that someone evidently thought would enhance the scene.

"Oh, vandal! What a horrible thing to do! I always like to think that no one comes here but us. Orange peel and banana skin, too! Put the turf back, Bianca. It's all scattered about. And I'll go and hide these in the bushes down there."

The hillside was very steep and perhaps she went too quickly. She didn't notice an almost hidden hole and suddenly jerked forward, wrenching her right leg very sharply. An agonizing pain shot from the back of her knee almost to her ankle and she shouted with dismay, landing in a tumbled heap.

The others were by her in a moment, startled by her white face.

"What is it, Drina? What have you done?"

"Pulled a muscle or something," Drina said, trying to sound calm, though the pain was still acute. "I caught my foot in a hole." She tried to rise, but found that she couldn't.

"It's all right. I shall be able to get up in a moment."

Petrouchka came to sniff at her anxiously, and the other three stood in a half-circle, silent and worried.

3

Drina in Trouble

"She's broke 'er leg!" Bianca cried at last. Her command of English still deserted her in a crisis.

"No," Drina said with difficulty. "I don't think it's that. It *felt* like a muscle. It seemed to rip all down the back of my leg. A horrible feeling!" She heaved herself up until she was sitting on the edge of the Cross, with her feet on the chalk.

Rose, looking very worried, said, "I expect it's the something or other muscle. The big one. Yvonne Darniar did it last term, running downhill."

"And what happened to her?" Drina asked sharply. Her first anxious thoughts had been for her dancing.

"Oh, she had to keep her leg up for a week or so; when she could, you know. She wasn't supposed to walk much."

"And her dancing?"

"Not for three weeks or a month," Rose said reluctantly.

"Oh, what hard luck!" Emilia, too, was very upset. "What shall we do, though? Go and ask them to bring a stretcher?"

At that Drina laughed.

"Can't you just see me being borne through Bledlow Great Wood on a stretcher? No, I'll be able to hobble soon. The worst of the pain's going off."

And, sure enough, in five minutes she was able to be

helped up the hillside and through the bushes on to the woodland path. But walking was certainly very painful. She could not put down her heel at all.

"I feel as though I need a four-inch heel on my right shoe," she said, making a courageous attempt to be cheerful, though she felt sick and afraid.

"But, Drina, ought you to try to walk?"

"I don't know, but I can't sit here waiting for a stretcher. That would be too idiotic."

"Then let Emilia and me make a chair," Rose insisted. "You aren't all that heavy. We can manage."

And in the end that was what they did, but they made slow progress and they were glad when they met the head gardener a couple of hundred yards from the Manor. He immediately picked Drina up and carried her into the house, while Rose flew for Matron.

Matron, on hearing the tale, looked grim.

"Yes, it sounds the same as Yvonne. Let me feel." And she ran quick fingers down the back of Drina's leg. She was a trained masseuse and well acquainted with muscles. "Hum! Can you walk at all? Then help her into Miss Sutherland's sitting-room, girls. We'd better find someone to take her to the station, and she must see her doctor as soon as she gets back to town."

"My dancing?" Drina gasped miserably.

"My dear, you'll not dance for some weeks, I'm pretty certain."

Matron sent the other girls off to look up the first train and to ask if Miss Crawford would run Drina to the station. Then she surveyed Drina thoughtfully.

"I'll make you a strong cup of tea. Cheer up, my dear! It isn't the end of the world."

"It will be if I can't dance for weeks," Drina said dismally.

"It's most unfortunate that it should happen. And it's

spoilt your day out, too." Then she asked quickly, "What made you come? Did Rose ask you to?"

Drina looked back into the shrewd eyes.

"No-o. I suggested it."

"Why? I know you're very fond of Rose, but you saw her only last week."

Drina hesitated and Matron went on, "She's not happy?"

"No-o, Matron. You see –" And then, since it seemed the ideal opportunity, and Drina guessed that Matron already suspected something, the story came out about Christine's unkind comments and downright snobbery. Matron looked grim during the telling.

"What I'm to do with that girl I do not know. I shall be glad when she leaves Chalk Green, though you can keep that to yourself. She made those poor girls in Markova miserable and I thought it was time they had a break. But she certainly can't be allowed to say such things to Rose. I detest snobbery. Now don't worry, Drina, and tell Rose not to. I'll see Miss Sutherland about it, and the only solution seems to be to give Christine a room to herself. There's that little boxroom on the first floor. If I put her in there she can only be unkind to herself."

"Oh, Matron, you *are* fantastic!" Drina cried, slightly happier to know that Rose's problem, at least, was solved.

"And Christine will get a good lecture. Worded strongly enough to keep her quiet for the whole of this term, at least. She's hopelessly spoilt and quite convinced that there's no one like Christine Gifford. Now I'll make you that cup of tea." And she bustled off.

Rose was allowed to go to the station in Miss Crawford's car, but there was no chance of private conversation then. However, Miss Crawford tactfully waited in the car, so they were able to have a few words before the train arrived.

"So you needn't worry," Drina told her, as they sat on a seat in the sun. "Matron will tell Miss Sutherland and you'll lose Christine."

"Oh, thank goodness!" Rose said fervently. "It was nice of you to tell her, Drina."

"I think she knew. She didn't seem surprised, only angry with Christine."

The train came then and Rose had to help Drina into it. Her face was still troubled as Drina leaned out of the window.

"I'm so *sorry* about your leg! It's all my fault."

"Rubbish! Of course it isn't. I'll survive, no doubt." But, as the train sped along the green valley towards High Wycombe, Drina felt very worried and unhappy indeed. She had planned to work so hard and every week counted, or so it seemed to her. She would find it little short of tragic if she had to stay away from the Dominick so near the beginning of term.

She was too unsettled to read, so she sat lost in dismal thoughts, her sandal off and her foot resting on the opposite seat. She hobbled along the platform at Marylebone and climbed into a taxi outside the station. Luckily she had enough money. When she reached the block of flats where she lived, she was thankful that there was a lift, for her leg ached badly and she still could not put her heel down properly.

When she heard the key in the lock Mrs Chester came hurrying out of the kitchen.

"You're very early. Why, Drina, what's the matter?"

But before Drina could reply she had slipped her arm round her granddaughter and led her to the comfortable sofa in the sitting-room.

"I knew I shouldn't have let you go alone. What have

you done to your leg?"

Drina managed to laugh.

"It would still have happened, Granny, if you and Grandfather had taken me in the car. I didn't do anything really. Just caught my foot in a hole near Bledlow Cross, and Matron said I'd pulled a muscle. I thought so myself at once. She said I must see a doctor."

Looking at her pale, distressed face, Mrs Chester clucked to herself.

"Well, I never did! What an unlucky thing! Just stay there quietly and I'll telephone the doctor now."

Luckily the doctor was in and he was with Drina in half an hour.

"Hum! Well, it's easily done. If you were old you'd have to lie up for some time. As it is, take things very easily. Keep your leg up when you can and don't try to walk much."

"What about school?" Mrs Chester asked.

"Oh, she'd better stay away for a week. After that she'll be able to walk pretty well, but the leg will be weak."

"But, doctor, you know I'm a dancer," Drina groaned, and he pulled her hair gently.

"I know. I've heard about it every time you've been ill. Making yourself worse with fretting. I never knew such a glutton for work. Well, you'll have to resign yourself. If you dance on that leg in less than three weeks or a month you'll have it all to do again. When you get back to the Dominick they'll probably arrange some massage or heat treatment for you. I'll get in touch with the doctor there."

"Oh, but – " It was just what Drina had expected, but the news was no easier to bear on that account.

"Bless you, girl! You'll be dancing with the best by

half-term. So grin and bear it." And he went off briskly.

"He's so horribly unsympathetic," Drina said, when her grandmother came back. "A week at home! A whole week! That means till a week on Monday. And then no dancing. I shall die!"

Mrs Chester brought in the tea and poured Drina out a cup. Her controlled face was rather grim. She disliked Drina's wild moods of happiness or despair and had always done her best to combat them.

"Really, Drina, I've wondered often what would happen if anything *really* terrible happened to you. Say you *lost* your leg in an accident, or broke your back, or any of the dreadful things that happen to people every day of the week?"

Drina looked at her with wide dark eyes.

"Oh, Granny, what awful ideas you have! I *should* die and that would be the end of it."

"Oh, no, you wouldn't. People rarely do. You'd bear it and find something else instead of dancing. Remember Adele Whiteway, who turned to designing when she couldn't dance any more."

"I've never known how she could bear it."

"Well, do stop looking so down in the dumps and show some ordinary courage."

"But – but fate is so unkind!"

"It could be a great deal more unkind, believe me. Surely you've learned by now that life isn't all honey and roses? I seem to be talking in clichés, but you'll have to learn to take the rough with the smooth."

"I do try. But things haven't always been easy for me."

"It's partly your temperament, and I suppose you can't help that really. You've been a lucky girl, all things considered. Most things have come to you, partly, I must admit, because you've set your teeth and fought for them. When I was fourteen I was looking after an invalid mother and helping to run a home, and I didn't have much fun and certainly no tastes of fame. So eat your tea and make the best of it."

Drina honestly did try, but the days ahead looked like an eternity to her. Life would be going on at the Dominick and she would not be there.

"Why don't you telephone Ilonka and ask her to come round?" Mrs Chester asked, about six o'clock.

Ilonka agreed readily and arrived soon after seven. She was very concerned to find Drina with her leg up and looking so dismal.

"Oh, but it is hard luck! And I shall miss you. All because you wished to help Rose."

"I did help her, anyway. She'll be all right now," Drina remarked and launched into an account of the day's happenings. Ilonka sat at the open window, listening intently. Then she said, "I also have news. You know it was said that Terza's book might be made into a play? Well, it is being done by Bertram Goldson-Wade – "

"But he's – he's one of the most famous modern English playwrights!"

"Yes. That I know. And he is so nice. Last night he came to the flat and talked to Terza for two, three hours."

"Oh, Ilonka, how exciting!"

"Yes," Ilonka agreed gravely. "Terza can hardly believe it. The play will be in three acts. The first in Lynzonia, in our flat – how strange it seems! Who would ever have thought that we would be in a play on the London stage?" And Ilonka's pale face looked very lost and thoughtful. Perhaps she was remembering those frightening days when Terza and her mother had gone and she was waiting to follow with her father.

"And the rest?"

"The second act with two scenes: one at the frontier and one in Vienna. And then London. An audition at the Dominick, and then the night of a performance of the ballet, when she learns that her sister is safe, but her father is not. That he may never come."

"Her sister? *You*, Ilonka!" And Drina had momentarily forgotten all about her leg. The story of the Lorencz family was something far greater and more tragic. How right her grandmother was!

Ilonka leaned on the window sill, her very black hair falling forward to hide her face.

"Yes."

"And you are to be in the first act?"

"Yes. A girl called Ilonka Lorencz. It will not be me, but an actress."

"But couldn't you do it yourself? You ought to. Wouldn't they let you?"

"I don't know, but I shouldn't wish. Neither would Terza. And there is to be – to be a cat – " Her voice faltered. Ilonka's beloved cat, that she had had to leave behind, was in the book but never before had she mentioned her.

"Oh, Ilonka!" Drina was suddenly so moved that she could have cried.

"A black cat with four white paws. Mitzi." Still Ilonka did not look up.

"Ilonka, you could have another cat. When you have the restaurant. Couldn't you?"

Ilonka looked up and there were tears on her thick black lashes.

"Yes, Mother says so. But I could never love another cat the same. Mitzi was so beautiful. I knew her so well and all she felt. She was so nervous, so afraid. She loved only us and we kept her safe. She will never have known – why we went away and left her there."

"But – someone would look after her?"

"Perhaps. Father gave her to a neighbour. But I shall feel guilty for ever because of Mitzi not understanding. It seems worse ... worse than all the death and trouble." Then she changed her tone abruptly. "But we have the restaurant. The papers are to be signed on Monday. You must come and see, Drina, as soon as you can walk."

"Of course I will," Drina agreed, and after that they talked about the Dominick until Ilonka had to leave at half-past nine.

The conversation about the play and Ilonka's tragic experiences had certainly helped Drina to find a sense of proportion, but, as she lay in bed after a hot bath, she felt very dismal indeed. It might not be a tragedy to anyone but herself, but it was going to be very hard to bear; not dancing for nearly a month. And all because she hated litter and was hiding someone else's disgusting orange peel and banana skin!

But it had been lovely in the Chilterns, and presently she fell asleep remembering the white froth of the hawthorn and the view from Lodge Hill, the smell of the grass, and the great curves of the beech-crowned ridges.

4

Dear Brutus

During the days that followed Drina was very restless and unsettled, especially as the weather was glorious and it irritated her to be indoors all the time. Mrs Chester insisted that she should get on with her schoolwork, and Ilonka arrived every evening to bring her the next day's assignment, taking away the lessons she had already done.

Jan Williams arrived with Ilonka on Tuesday evening, bringing a box of chocolates and several magazines. He was very sorry about Drina's enforced inactivity and could sympathize, as he had sprained his ankle very badly skating that winter.

Wednesday found Ilonka with another companion, Igor Dominick, also bearing chocolates and some French magazines. Mrs Chester, though she made little comment, was amused by the contrast between the two boys: Jan so sturdy and British, and Igor, taller and so strikingly handsome, with his long lashes and his rather adult manner. Igor was very charming to Mrs Chester and she could see his subtle resemblance to his father, whom she had known quite well in the days when her daughter Betsy had achieved great fame as Elizabeth Ivory.

"He certainly has a good opinion of himself," she said, a little acidly, when Igor and Ilonka had gone. "I can see how he got everyone's back up last term. But he's going to be a handsome man, and I daresay a clever one."

"I like Igor," Drina said serenely. "And he can't help his manner. He's getting quite popular now, Ilonka says. They're beginning to admire him. At first most people could have hit him."

"And he doesn't know that your mother was Ivory? I didn't like to say that I knew his father."

"Certainly not, Granny!" Drina cried, horrified. "I wouldn't *dream* of telling him!"

"I don't know how you've managed to keep the secret for so long. I wouldn't have believed it possible."

"I shall keep it a lot longer," Drina said firmly. "I will *not* be noticed because my mother was great and famous! If I can't manage on my own – "

"It seems to me you're managing pretty well," her grandmother said, with a touch of grim approval, and marched out to prepare the evening meal.

When Drina's grandfather arrived home, he was carrying a large and apparently heavy parcel in his arms and a green and grey case dangled from one supporting hand.

"Here, Drina! Take the case. Be careful. They're records. There's more outside. It's a record player!"

Drina gasped and then seized the case, while he unpacked the parcel on the table.

"Something to keep you quiet," he said.

"Oh, Grandfather! I have so longed to have my own. I've been saving up, as you know."

"Then keep your money for new records. It's time you had something more modern than that old gramophone. See if the records are to your taste. I got all ballet music, but probably you'd like to get some orchestral ones, or opera. You may have some already."

"I'd like some Beethoven and Mozart," Drina said,

eagerly opening the case. "But I haven't come round to opera yet. Ballet never seems silly, though I know it has its own conventions, but opera does: all those large men and women taking such a long time to die. Still, I shall have to get to know more about it when the Dominick Opera Company starts, as it may do early next year. Oh, *Grandfather*! that new recording of *Les Sylphides*! I do love the music so. It's still my favourite ballet. And two records of *The Sleeping Beauty* . . . *Casse Noisette* . . . *Carnival* . . . *Giselle*. Oh, how marvellous of you! What's this?" And she drew out a record with a strange orange motif on the sleeve. "*Solitaire* – to Arnold's English Dances."

"I didn't know if you'd seen that," Mr Chester said doubtfully. "Of course it's very modern, but the girl said it was a wonderful recording."

"No, it hasn't been danced for quite a while. But I've read about it. It's meant to be a kind of game for one. The Girl keeps on joining in with the others, but at the end of each dance she's quite alone again. I heard the music once on the radio. It was very old and very modern mixed. I've longed to hear it again and get to know it better. Perhaps they'll revive the ballet some time. There was a strange set, kind of thin scaffolding, and, at the beginning, a sort of orange flag hanging down near the front of the stage."

"I'm glad you're pleased," said Mr Chester, a little bewildered by the flood of information. "You know I hate you to be ill or unhappy."

Drina spent the evening listening to the new records and, though she felt a little wistful that she could not dance, she was happier than she had been for some days. The *Solitaire* music seemed to grow on her more each time she heard it, and when she had played it three times Mrs Chester protested.

"That's too modern for me, I'm afraid. All those discords."

"But it's so wonderfully dancy, too! I think it's the most exciting music I've heard for ages. It even makes *Les Sylphides* seem a bit – sugary."

By the weekend Drina's leg was much better and she could walk almost normally. But she was still in low spirits, feeling that she was wasting her precious time.

Then on Sunday morning she read a small item in the newspaper that gave her considerable food for thought. The paragraph read:

"Mr Calum Campbell, the well-known theatrical producer, tells me that he has had great ill-luck over his forthcoming production of Barrie's Dear Brutus, *which is billed to follow* The Admirable Crichton *in a fortnight's time. After some initial difficulty in finding a suitable Margaret, he engaged the young actress Sybil Sarlow. But last night Miss Sarlow was in hospital undergoing an operation for acute appendicitis. Since rehearsals were about to start tomorrow this is quite a problem.*

"Marla Lerieu is to play Alice Dearth and Clement Chandos Mr Dearth, the father of Margaret who 'might have been'. Mr Campbell tells me that Barrie's plays are good box-office and he is especially anxious to put on Dear Brutus."

Drina put down the paper quietly and shut herself up in her own room with her copy of Barrie's plays. When her grandmother looked in half an hour later, she was sitting on the floor in a patch of sunlight, with tears pouring down her cheeks.

Mrs Chester was startled.

"Really, Drina! What is it *now*?"

"It's nothing, Granny. Just something I'm reading," Drina said hastily, and her grandmother went off with a disgusted cluck. To cry at all was bad enough, but to cry over a book was, to her, the height of sentimental

folly. But Drina had found herself quite lost in the second act in the mysterious wood, where Mr Dearth was so happy with Margaret. It was so terrible when he saw the lights of the house and insisted on leaving Margaret alone.

Margaret alone in the darkening wood ... rushing from tree to tree ... knowing that she did not really exist.

Drina saw herself there, in that wood, and felt all the sorrow. She heard her own voice ringing out in those words:

"Daddy, come back; I don't want to be a might-have-been!"

Poor Mrs Chester! Before lunch she was surprised to find Drina in the kitchen balancing a biscuit on her nose and doing her best to toss it up into the air and catch it. The biscuit hit Drina sharply in the eye and she gave a gasp of pain.

"Oh, Drina! What *is* the matter with you this morning? Why do such a silly thing?"

Drina leaned against the kitchen table, still blinking.

"It's all right, Granny. I haven't gone mad. I was being Margaret."

"Margaret?"

"Yes, you know. In *Dear Brutus*. Catching biscuits was a trick she had when she was little and she's showing her father that she can still do it. Granny, I think I may try for the part after all."

"Why?" Mrs Chester asked doubtfully, not looking best pleased.

"Because the girl who got the part is in hospital with appendicitis and rehearsals are supposed to begin tomorrow. I've just read it in the paper. I suppose they can get on with the first and third acts, but they'll have to have a Margaret. Granny, could I telephone Mr

Campbell?"

"At his home, do you mean?"

"I suppose so. I don't suppose he's at the theatre today. I can get the number out of the telephone book, or perhaps it was on his letter. I still have it somewhere."

"But I thought you'd decided not to act?"

"So I did, but now I can't dance for a while I may as well have the part if possible. It would mean rehearsing for a fortnight and acting for a fortnight, and by then my leg will be quite better. Probably long before. Margaret does actually do a little dance in the wood, but I could manage that quite soon. It'd only be a few impromptu movements."

"Well, if you must you must," said Mrs Chester resignedly.

Calum Campbell exclaimed in deepest relief when he heard Drina's tale about not being able to dance and being willing to try for the part.

"My dear girl, you're pretty nearly an answer to a prayer. Can you come over to my house this afternoon? We had the dress rehearsal for *Crichton* yesterday, so I'm free. I can run through Dearth's part with you."

"Oh, yes, I expect so. I'll ask Grandfather to drive me to Hampstead."

"Three o'clock, then, and bless you. Thank heaven you pulled that muscle, though I'm sure you don't agree."

Well, it was pleasant to be so enthusiastically received by such a well-known producer, but Drina certainly did not completely agree with him.

Mr Chester did drive her to the Hampstead house that afternoon and he and his wife walked on the Heath and sat in the sun during the two hours that

Drina was with Calum Campbell.

When she reappeared she was flushed and excited.

"I got it! He says he thinks I'll make a very appealing Margaret. But just think! I shall be playing opposite Clement Chandos. I've only seen him in films. I shall be terrified."

"I don't see why you should be," said Mr Chester calmly. "Mr Campbell obviously thinks you're good."

"And now, I suppose, we've got all the trouble of renewing your licence and finding out if Miss Thorne can be with you in the theatre," Mrs Chester remarked.

Drina pulled a face. "It's idiotic. I don't need anyone. Who makes the stupid rules?"

"I'm sure you know quite well, and they're made, I suppose, to protect children who are in pantomimes and so on."

"Still, I can get on with my schoolwork quite well by myself, and anyway Mr Campbell says it won't mean missing very much school. He'll arrange the rehearsals of the second act so that they're fairly late in the afternoon. Of course, there'll be the lighting rehearsal and the dress rehearsal, but *that* will probably be on a Sunday."

On Monday morning, Drina went back to the Dominick School, to be met by commiserating comments from Betty and Jill, Lorna and Meryl.

"But you need not be too sorry for her," said Ilonka cheerfully. "She is to act opposite Clement Chandos." Ilonka had already learned a good deal about British stage people and she had seen Clement Chandos in a film only the previous week.

They all gaped and Queenie gave an unfriendly snort.

"A likely story!"

Ilonka flushed. She was not in the least afraid of

Queenie and she thought her airs ridiculous.

"You are always so disbelieving, Queenie. It is the truth."

"It can't be."

"It's true enough," Drina said quietly. They were all changing into their practice clothes, while she had no need to, not being able to dance. "I have to rest my leg for a time, so I applied for the part and got it. Margaret in *Dear Brutus*."

"It's a terribly dated play," Queenie said nastily. "All Barrie's are. I can't think why Calum Campbell is bothering."

"What about *Peter Pan*? That goes on for ever. Besides, he's very keen about Barrie and thinks the plays still good box office. I love *Dear Brutus* myself."

"We will all come and see you," said Ilonka.

Drina was not expected at the theatre that morning, so she did her school work as usual, but that afternoon, at half-past two, she met Miss Thorne in Kingsway and they walked the short distance to the Queen Elizabeth Theatre. Miss Thorne was pleased to see Drina again. She had really retired from her work as chaperone to stage children, but she had accompanied Drina's mother when she was young and felt it impossible to refuse Mrs Chester's request. Besides it would only be for a short time, and Drina was an easy pupil.

Drina herself thought it absurd that she must have a chaperone, but she was fond of Miss Thorne and found her stories about stage children most fascinating.

As they approached the stage door she hung back for a moment.

"I'm scared! Scared of facing them all. Suppose I'm no good, after all?"

Miss Thorne said reassuringly, "Of course you'll be good."

The moment they greeted the stage door man Drina felt better, more confident. The old man remembered her and greeted her with pleasure.

She followed Miss Thorne along the passages, sniffing as she went.

"Oh, it hits me each time – the lovely, lovely smell of a theatre!"

Miss Thorne stopped and looked at her. Her wrinkled old face looked tired and rather disillusioned, but her eyes were kind.

"It's a cold, dusty smell. I can't say I've ever liked it."

"Yes. I know. And greasepaint, and wood; a thousand things. In an odd way I think the smell of greasepaint and sweat *are* the theatre."

Miss Thorne, who would have thought it more ladylike to say "perspiration", continued on her way and soon they emerged on to the stage. There was only a harsh working light overhead and the scenery for the first act of that evening's production of *The Admirable Crichton* was already in place. A number of people were talking over on the prompt side and Calum Campbell detached himself from them as soon as he saw Drina.

"There you are, Drina! Good afternoon, Miss Thorne. We've read through the first and third acts and are ready to start on the second. Tomorrow we'll concentrate on the moves. Now come and meet the others. Marla Lerieu you know, I think?"

"Yes, of course we know each other," the well-known actress said cheerfully, for she had been in *Argument in Paris*.

"It's nice to see you again," Drina murmured shyly. "I – I often wondered what happened to your daughter. Has she left her boarding-school in the country?"

"She has," the actress said ruefully. "She beat me in

the end. She's making a film at the moment. Only a small part, but a good one. I never wanted her to be an actress."

Calum Campbell led Drina on, giving a tall, dark man a slap on the back.

"Clement, here's your Margaret!"

Clement Chandos turned slowly and Drina saw that he was certainly not so young as he looked in films. But he had an interesting face and a friendly smile.

"Hullo, Drina. I can tell you we've been in a state! We're very glad to see you."

"Wasn't there an understudy?" Drina asked. She had meant to ask Mr Campbell the previous afternoon, but had forgotten.

"No. But we think we've got one now."

A girl of nineteen or twenty came quickly out of the prompt corner and seized Drina's hand.

"*Well!* You haven't grown much, I must say. You look just the same as you did in *Argument*. Twelve, were you?"

"Thirteen," Drina said, clasping the long, thin hand warmly. "Oh, Lally, how have you been getting on?"

"Not too badly," said Lally Devine, who had been greatly upset when *Argument in Paris*, her first real chance, had not run. "A bit of everything – film work, radio, television, even pantomime in the provinces. Funny that we should come together again."

"Who are you playing? Lady Caroline?"

"Wather," said Lally, and they both laughed. In the play Lady Caroline could not say her "r's".

"Oh, Lally, I'm so glad!"

"So am I," the young actress said rather grimly. "I thought I'd struck a bad patch and was down to my last five pounds again. What a life! Are you still keenest on dancing?"

"Oh, of course. But I've strained a muscle and can't dance for the moment. But, oh, Lally! I danced with the Dominick in Genoa. Just for one night, but it was the thrill of my life."

"And I saw your photograph in the *Standard*. Oh, well, to work!"

"You haven't met the others," said Calum Campbell waving his hand round, reeling off a list of names and the parts they were playing. Not all were familiar to Drina, but she looked very sharply at the little old man who was to play Lob. Caradoc Lee! She had heard of him, of course, if only because her grandparents had talked of him, but she had thought him probably dead. He had been great and famous in his day and now must be at least eighty, surely? He looked so remarkably as she had imagined Lob that she was startled. That puckish face, mischievous eyes, long nose and small, thin, still pliant body! No better Lob could ever have been found, she was convinced.

As Lally and the man who was playing Matey took their places to start the second act, the old man murmured in Drina's ear, "Like the play, do you? Campbell told me it was one of your favourites."

"I love it," Drina said warmly. "That moment when they draw the curtains back at the end of the first act and the wood is there, where the garden has been! Every time I read it my skin prickles."

"Nearly as good theatre as that moment in *Outward Bound* when they all find they're dead," he agreed. "This will be the third time I've played Lob. Just suits me, everyone tells me!" And his bright eyes twinkled at her.

"Oh, it does! I mean," Drina added hastily, "I'm sure you'll be very good." But even that sounded wrong. Of course he would be good. She flushed and felt awkward, but he twinkled at her again.

"I'm not past it yet! I'm making a film, starting next month. The village idiot."

"Really?" She was not sure if he was pulling her leg.

"Well, the oldest inhabitant; a hundred and one. Actually I'm only eighty-one, but a bit of make-up will do the trick!"

Then the act started and Drina stood to one side, thinking of the play, thinking of Margaret and Barrie's words: "She is as lovely as you think she is, and she is aged the moment you like your daughter best."

As the reading went on Drina thought, with a surge of wonder, that this was the beginning. Something was to be created, a transient magic that would die for ever when the curtain came down for the last time. No production of any play was ever the same, the special magic was never quite recreated. It seemed to her, as it had seemed over *Argument in Paris*, that it was a pity that it was so ephemeral a thing, so soon lost and forgotten. But that was the theatre. It was not like a book that you could hold in your hands, or a painting, or even a film. It was a brief reality, born of different personalities, of the set, of the producer's ideas.

Drina had read the play so often that she almost knew her part already, but this was only a reading and she did not have to race on to the stage ahead of her father.

At first she was shy and nervous, intimidated by the knowledge of Clement Chandos's importance. Apparently he had only agreed to play Dearth between film work. "To keep my hand in on the stage," she had heard him saying just now to the man who was playing Mr Coade.

But it seemed to Drina that there was not the slightest need for him to keep his hand in. It was in already, that was clear. Even reading the part he was dynamic and before they had gone very far Drina was Margaret in spirit. The old magic was back with a vengeance and the Dominick seemed to have receded.

"It'll do," the producer said at last. "Now we'll just run through Act Three again. You can hop off, Drina. I'm sure you want your tea. Same time tomorrow."

Drina parted from Miss Thorne in Kingsway and set off briskly towards the river. It was after five o'clock, so there was no chance of meeting anyone from the Dominick.

Though she *did* want her tea she walked all the way, climbing down on to the Embankment close to Waterloo Bridge. Her grandmother appeared in the hall when she heard the key in the lock.

"Oh, you're back, Drina! Goodness, how flushed you look"!

"I walked fast, and I'm still excited, Granny," Drina cried, and Mrs Chester shook her head doubtfully. Certainly Drina looked a different girl from the drooping, bored one who had been about the flat for over a week. That was the worst of it: she was always either up or down, never in ordinary spirits.

"Walked fast? What about your leg?"

"Good gracious!" said Drina frankly. "I forgot all about it. It must be better. Better for walking, anyway. I'm to have heat treatment and so on while the others are having their ballet classes."

"Good. And how did the rehearsal go?"

"Oh, we just read through the play." Drina went and stood by the window in the sun, her hands on the sill. "I can see it's going to 'get' me. I do love it so. And everyone was so nice, even Clement Chandos. He's going to be wonderful as Mr Dearth. And, Granny, guess who's playing Lob!"

"How could I?"

"Caradoc Lee, and he's exactly right. Ageless and fairy-like. Mischievous. Of course he isn't in the second act, but they'd started Act Three again before I left. They were really only reading, but he insisted on being asleep in a chair – or pretending to be, you know. Really Lob is quite aware of what's going on."

"Well, fancy!" said Mrs Chester. "Your grandfather will be interested. Lee must be very old."

"Eighty-one, he said. Oh, Granny, it was so – so superb to be back in a theatre. I love the atmosphere and the people and – oh, everything!"

"And you've forgotten to worry about your dancing?"

Drina turned round.

"I did forget. Now I think I'm *glad* that things have happened this way. But I'm almost afraid that acting will get a hold on me. Because really and truly there's nothing in the world but ballet."

5

Drina the Actress

For the rest of that week life settled down to the hours at the Dominick and the ones on the stage at the Queen Elizabeth Theatre. The hard work suited Drina and she felt very happy. The play was rapidly taking shape, most of them were nearly word perfect and the magic – in spite of the working light overhead, the occasional tempers of the producer, and dissatisfactions of the players – increased for Drina with every day that passed. It was the growth of the play that fascinated her, the gradual building up and shaping, the extraordinary way in which the printed words and instructions leaped into vivid life.

For the most part she did not have to waste much time, for she arrived in time for the second act and was generally able to leave when it was over. But if the producer wanted a later run-through she got on with her schoolwork in one of the dressing-rooms, though she longed to stay in the wings and watch what was going on.

On the Thursday of that week Rose wrote a long letter about events at Chalk Green.

"As I told you," she wrote, *"Christine was simply wild at first, but she didn't dare to say much after the lecture she got. Sue (or Joan, I never know which) told me that she thinks Miss Sutherland told her she would have to leave before the*

end of term if she couldn't behave herself. So now she contents herself with just glaring every time we meet. I try not to mind, but it makes me very uncomfortable.

"Anyway, we've settled down very happily with Bronwen Williams, Jan's little cousin. I always liked her, and Bianca loves her. They are very good friends. Bronwen often makes us laugh. She's quite a mimic and marches up and down Ivory in just her vest and knickers imitating Matron and Christine and different members of the staff.

"Oh, Drina, everywhere looks so lovely. The hawthorn isn't over yet and it just foams everywhere. The scent is overpowering. And the wild flowers are coming out along the Icknield Way. I found some of those Common Twayblades in Bledlow Great Wood yesterday – sort of orchids, aren't they? You remember? We identified them last year.

"Emilia and Bianca and the twins all send their love and good wishes for Dear Brutus. And, I nearly forgot to tell you, Miss Sutherland offered to get a block of seats for the half-past five performance on the first Saturday because we all know you. All our class leaped at it, except for Christine, of course. So we're coming up. Won't it be exciting?"

Well, it would certainly be exciting for the party from Chalk Green – they always looked forward to any trip to London – but the thought of them coming to a performance made Drina decidedly nervous. She felt that she didn't mind any ordinary audience, but it made her spine tingle when she remembered how many of her friends and acquaintances from the Dominick had told her they were going to see the play. Some, like Queenie, would go just to criticize unkindly, and others would be genuinely sympathetic and interested.

Marianne Volonaise, meeting Drina and Ilonka in Red Lion Square one morning, smiled in a friendly way and asked, "How's the play going, Drina? It was a good idea of yours to take the part while you can't dance. Though I hear that your leg will soon be strong again."

"Oh! I – I think it's going quite well, Madam."

"I shall come and see it, of course. I've always been fond of *Dear Brutus*, and with one of our own students as Margaret – "

Drina's face was so appalled that she laughed.

"My dear child, what's the matter? You didn't mind me seeing you dance."

"No-o. But acting is different. I love being Margaret, but – but I don't know how good I shall be."

"It's a difficult part. Deceptively simple, but not all that easy to pull off. But I'm sure you'll be good. I haven't forgotten *Argument*."

"She speaks to you like – like a friend," Ilonka said, as the two went on.

"She's very nice," Drina answered. "But she *isn't* a friend and I wish she'd stay away from *Dear Brutus*. It makes me feel awful to think of it."

At the bottom of the cloakroom stairs she came face to face with young Igor Dominick, who grinned and remarked, "And how's the actress? My father has taken three seats for the second night."

Drina groaned.

"Oh, *not* your father, too! Miss Volonaise has just told me she's coming."

"She is going with us. Why should you mind?"

"Because I care so enormously what they think, I suppose," Drina confessed, but her spirits soon revived. After all, you could not be in a West End play without an audience, and it was nice of the great ones to be so interested.

That evening she wrote to Jenny Pilgrim. She had not seen Jenny for quite a long time, but that never made the slightest difference to their friendship. Jenny was her dearest and closest friend, unchanging, warm and very understanding. Their interests were quite different, for Jenny's whole heart was in farming, but she knew all about Drina's hopes and fears. In fact, Drina told her many things that she could not have confessed to anyone else.

"Oh, Jenny, I do wish we could meet," she wrote. *"I just long to have one of our long talks, preferably in our pyjamas before going to bed. Please, please try to come up for the last weekend of the play. I've got you a seat for the second performance on the last Saturday, just in case, and Granny and Grandfather will be going then, too, as well as on the first night. Most people I know I rather dread, but* you *– please ask your mother if you can come.*

"I am terribly caught up in it and each day it gets more real. Lob is marvellous. Today I got there when they were still on the first act. Oh, I do so long for the dress rehearsal, to see the real set and the moment when the curtains are drawn back and the magic wood is there, crowding up against the house. It's the sort of play that does make you think. They all want a second chance, and yet when they get it in the wood they mostly go the same way. Mr Dearth, of course, is much nicer, because he has his Margaret, and Mr Coade is lovely – capering about so happily, playing his whistle.

"By the time the play opens I can probably start dancing again, and that will be a relief, as, at the back of my mind, I'm very conscious of wasting time.

"Have you been to the farm lately? By the way, I met Philip the other day in Kingsway, looking so grown up and quite different from the way he looked in Wales when he took us climbing. It must be odd to have brothers and such a grown up one. But I suppose it will be years yet before he is a doctor."

And Jenny wrote back by return:

"Dear Drina,

"I told Mother I'd just got to see you in Dear B. *and she groaned about the fare, but of course agreed. She says for two pins she'd come up herself, but we're having a visitor that weekend. I rather wish she could come, as she doesn't seem quite herself lately, almost as though she's worrying about something. I've felt the same about Father. Anyway, you certainly can't be in a play without my seeing you. I think* Dear B. *is a bit soppy, especially the Margaret part and 'not wanting to be a might-have-been, Daddy', but I know you'll be very good. I shall clap loudly and tell everyone within hearing that you're my sister! You are, too, in everything that counts.*

"Yes, I had a weekend at the farm. It was wonderful. I cleaned out the pigs, whitewashed the dairy and milked three times. There are four dear little new-born Hereford calves. You'd love them. You remember the next farm – Hogdens'? Run by an old couple who are very nice? Well it seems that their son and his wife have been killed in a motoring accident and the son – their grandson – is coming to live at the farm. He's said to be nineteen and he's been in an office, but hated it. And who wouldn't? He's called Robert Hogden; not very interesting or romantic, is it? But I suppose I shall meet him some time, and it will be nice to have a younger neighbour there.

"By the way, I met Mark the other day and he seems very torn about leaving Willerbury and going to the Dominick. I think he's been teased a lot, but he does want to be a dancer. I suppose he must be good. His mother has found him a room in Bloomsbury with some Willerbury people. His aunt has left London."

"Yes, Phil wrote to Mother and told her that he'd met you. For your edification he said, 'Drina Adams is a real good-

looker, and she moves better than any other girl I've ever seen.' How's that for a compliment from the superior Philip?"

In fact, it seemed to Drina a very great compliment, but she was surprised, for Philip had not seemed particularly approachable and she had been shy of him, conscious of his importance in his own eyes.

She was delighted that Jenny was coming to London, and the knowledge that she would be there on the last night of the play was very comforting. For, inevitably, it would be sad to know that the curtain had come down for the last time. Drina took no offence over Jenny's comments about *Dear Brutus*. When it came to the point she would probably enjoy the play.

So the days passed and the play was whole – each movement and entrance beautifully timed, each speech given its proper significance. And at last it was time to go to the dress rehearsal.

It was a great thrill to see the set for the first act and to find the backstage regions humming with carpenters, stage hands and electricians. Drina watched the first act from the front of the Circle, sitting in solitary state, for she was the only one not in that act. Down in the stalls were quite a number of people; friends of the cast, members of the management, a few reporters and critics. But, though there was a sprinkling of people in the Circle, there was no one near her.

She sat with clasped hands, forgetting to be nervous as her pleasure increased. The act went almost without a hitch and then, at last, the moment for which she had been waiting came – the moment when the wood was there, dim and menacing in the moonlight. One by one they ventured out through the window, leaving Lob alone. Then Matey came in with a tray of coffee cups.

"It's past your bedtime, Sir. Say goodnight to the

ladies and come along."

The strange little figure of Lob looked very small and puckish.

"Matey, look!"

"Good heavens! Then it's true!"

"Yes, but I – I wasn't sure."

Then, as Matey approached the window to peer out, Lob gave him the sudden push that propelled him into the wood. Lob stood alone, frightened and yet excited, and the curtain came softly down.

Drina rose and flew for the pass door, for it was time for her to get ready. She was already made up, but she had to put on Margaret's slightly old-fashioned dress. The moment had nearly come; this time there would be a real wood, and not the set for *The Admirable Crichton*. Excitement and fear took her by the throat and she felt for a short while that she could not breathe.

"You'll miss all the excitement when the play's over," said Mrs Chester, when Drina returned from the dress rehearsal, bright-eyed, flushed and ravenously hungry. "I don't at all know whether it's good for you."

"Oh, I think it is," Drina said cheerfully. By this time she was used to her grandmother's fits of gloomy doubt and disapproval. "I'm enjoying every moment of it, even when I'm scared to death."

"It seems a strange way of enjoying yourself."

"Well, you know what I mean. I enjoy it all; being with stage people, and counting as one of them, having my photograph taken – it's up in the foyer already, Granny, I saw it just now – hearing all the stage hands and electricians talking about battens and flats, dim-outs, blackouts, the iron, and all the rest. I like having a dressing-room to myself – except for my understudy, of course. I'd just *hate* to be an understudy; it must be so

dull. And Sally minds – not like Bernadette in *Argument*.
Bernadette said it was a rest, but Sally told me frankly
she almost wished I'd get a sore throat or something."

"That wasn't very kind of her."

"Oh, I don't blame her in the least, but I *mustn't* get a
sore throat, all the same. Mr Campbell told me in
confidence that she isn't very good, but he couldn't get
anyone better. Isn't that odd when you think of all the
girls who are mad to go on the stage? As for missing it
afterwards – well, I minded bitterly when *Argument*
finished, because I thought it would run for months,
but I know this will only be for two weeks. There'll still
be about a month of term left and I must work like
anything. And, of course, I start dancing again
tomorrow. But I'm to take things easily."

"I don't believe you know how to," said Mrs Chester
ruefully.

"Oh, I will. I don't want to bust that muscle again. It
gave me a horrible fright. When *Dear Brutus* is over I
shall really start working hard again. Ilonka will be
glad to have me back. I think she's missing me. We
haven't seen so much of each other lately. Usually
we're together after school. Do you know, I've only
seen her father once. I was a little scared of him. He
seems a dear, but he doesn't speak much English yet,
and he looks so old and – and worn. Nearly as old as
Grandfather somehow."

"Poor man!" said Mrs Chester. "I'm not surprised
after all he's been through. Have they got the
restaurant yet?"

"Oh, yes, it's all fixed up and they're moving next
Thursday. I haven't even been to see it, but I shall go
after school one day. I'll be more free once the play
starts."

"Well, don't go tearing round getting tired. You

ought to come home and have a good rest before the performance. One thing, you won't be home very late at night, not being in the third act."

Mrs Chester would have given a very great deal, she often told herself, for Drina to be leading a different life, the life of an ordinary schoolgirl, perhaps interested in games and riding and going to a musical show or a pantomime as a special treat. Instead Drina despised musicals, as much as she could despise anything to do with the theatre, would not dream of going to a pantomime, and was reading and insisting on seeing when possible what Mrs Chester considered to be quite unsuitable plays. Probably, at fourteen, she did not understand all of them, but she appeared to do so and always read the theatre critics in the *Sunday Times* and the *Observer*. Lately, since her return from Italy, she had not seen quite so much ballet as usual, apart from the visits to the Dominick Theatre with the school, but she had several times asked to be taken to new plays.

"If only she'd stick to Barrie and – and Shakespeare," Mrs Chester had said to her husband, but he had only laughed.

"She has an enquiring mind and wants to read and see all kinds. You used to complain when her interests didn't extend beyond ballet."

"But she's only fourteen. When I was her age I'd scarcely seen more than pantomime and *Where the Rainbow Ends*."

"She'll be fifteen in the autumn and it can't harm her. I expect a lot goes over her head. I'm sure it does over mine."

At all events, that Sunday night before *Dear Brutus* opened, Drina's mind was entirely given over to Barrie. She was possessed by thoughts of the play and her whole being was a mixture of excitement and cold fear.

In less than twenty-four hours. . . . in twenty-one and a half, to be exact, the curtain would go up and she would again be facing a critical first-night audience. Because she loved her part so much she wanted desperately to be thought good, and also it would be very hard to face the Dominick if she got bad notices. She fell asleep haunted by Queenie's triumphant face and dreamed that she was late for the theatre . . . that when she finally arrived at the stage door Sally was standing there in Margaret's costume, saying over and over again: "Too late! Too late! This is my chance!"

Drina awoke feeling tired and uneasy, but dared not let her grandmother know. So she set off at her usual time, not cheered by the fact that it was a wet morning and very cold for June. Passing buses and cars sent up great sprays of dirty water and people had a dismal air as they stood at the bus-stops.

But once at the Dominick, changing into her practice clothes, Drina felt better and soon she had no thoughts to spare for the play. It was good to be dancing again, though she felt that she had lost ground, and of course there was never any chance to think during lessons. She stayed for lunch in the canteen, as she usually did during summer, and Ilonka, who stayed too, was eager to talk about "The Golden Zither".

"Oh, Drina, it is looking so lovely! The sign is done and there is to be a gold and white awning. All the cloths are goldy-yellow and the same artist who did the sign is going to do some wall paintings. Oh, Drina, you will come soon?"

"Yes, honestly I will. Just as soon as the play really gets started." The *play* . . . for a moment Drina's stomach felt frighteningly unsteady and she looked with dislike at the biscuits and cheese she had just fetched to have with her coffee.

"All will be well," said Ilonka warmly. "You will be good, Drina. Never fear."

Once again Drina pushed thoughts of the evening away and the afternoon, surprisingly, passed quickly. She was sped from the Dominick School with many good wishes and Ilonka walked to the bottom of Kingsway with her. By then the rain had stopped, though it was still very grey, so Drina walked back to Westminster along the Embankment, occasionally pausing to look down at the water. How odd life was! How terribly odd! Things happened that you had scarcely dreamed of . . . you became an actress almost without effort when you wanted more than anything in the world to know that you would be a dancer.

She went on rapidly and Big Ben struck half-past four as she approached Westminster Bridge.

Two and a half hours later she was in the theatre, opening her big pile of letters and cards. And life was entirely dreamlike.

6
Acting or Dancing?

There was a characteristic card from Jenny that did much to make Drina happy.

"Thinking of you being a might-have-been. Love, Sister Jenny."

"Oh, Jenny!" Drina thought. "How like you!"

The quarter hour was called, five minutes, overture and beginners. The time seemed to have flown between each call. Drina ventured out on to the stage and found Lally at her side, tense and nervous.

"Oh, how I hate a first night! I shall dry up; I know I shall. The critics will be awful."

"I almost wish that Sally could go on instead of me," Drina agreed. She was very frightened and yet deeply excited too. She did not really wish that Sally could take her place. Probably everything would be all right when the play started.

She stood in the wings throughout the first act, gradually forgetting her tension as she sensed that the audience was held. There was a deep silence beyond the footlights as the act moved on towards the moment when the wood would be there, beyond the huge window. And though Drina knew very well that the trees were on painted canvas, moved into place by the stagehands, the knowledge did nothing to spoil her own thrill. The wood was Lob's wood; the magic wood that was said to appear somewhere in the usually

almost treeless country on Midsummer's Eve. And Lob was only himself: the little ageless half-man, half-fairy.

When the curtain came down after the first act Lally rushed to her.

"It went well! They liked it. Beforehand I was almost wishing that I worked in an office, but now everything's all right."

"Don't forget the critics," said the woman who was playing Joanna.

"I haven't. We'll have to face them in the morning. But just now I don't care."

The scene-changing went on rapidly and soon the drawing-room had given place to the woodland glade. Clement Chandos, meeting Drina in a passage, put his hand on her bony shoulder.

"Not scared, daughter?"

"A bit," Drina confessed.

"No need to be. They always fall for Margaret. She *is* the daughter they had or might have had. The thought touches everyone's heart."

"Will it touch the critics' hearts?" Drina asked, and he laughed.

"There you have me. Have critics got hearts? One doubts it."

When the moment came to go racing on to the stage Drina's fear had gone and she was already lost in the play. The sea of faces in the darkened auditorium meant nothing to her. She *was* Margaret throughout the scene, putting up her hair, using a pool as a looking-glass, Margaret balancing the biscuit on her nose – and catching it, too! – Margaret alone at last and aware of her own unreality.

"Daddy, come back! I don't want to be a might-have-been."

The downward swish of the curtain found her dazed

and shaken, almost as though she, too, had no reality. But, back in her dressing-room, she gradually returned to the real world. Miss Thorne, her grandparents and Ilonka (who had been taken by the Chesters) were all there, eagerly congratulating her. That is to say, everyone was eager but Mrs Chester, who merely said quietly, "I thought you were quite good. Really quite moving." But that was high praise from Drina's calm, self-contained grandmother.

Drina was allowed to stay until the final curtain that evening, and she again watched as the wanderers in the wood returned gradually to Lob's house, where Lob himself lay twitching and pretending to sleep in his chair. Then, when it was all over, she joined the rest of the cast as the curtain rose and fell again and again. Whatever the critics might say in the morning it seemed that the first-night audience liked the play.

Ten minutes later, in her own clothes but still wearing her make-up, she was met at the stage door by her grandparents and was whirled home through the still light streets. The June evening had, amazingly, turned sunny, and the sunset was spreading across the western sky.

"Bed!" said Mrs Chester, as soon as Drina had finished her milk and biscuits. "Or you'll never be up in time for school." And Drina kissed them both and went to her own little room. She might be an actress – temporarily, at any rate – but she was still obedient to her grandmother's brisk commands.

Drina was awake early and had shot out into the hall in her pyjamas only a moment or two after the papers arrived, a big bundle of them, especially ordered by Mr Chester.

Mrs Chester looked out to say rather crossly, "Really, Drina! You'll get cold. It seems really chilly this morning. Can't the papers wait?"

"If I don't see them now I shan't have time," said Drina and dashed back to bed, clutching the bundle to her chest.

To her disappointment there was not a great deal about *Dear Brutus*, though most papers gave it a few lines. One critic said that it was time Barrie was dropped, as his plays were too sentimental for present-day audiences, but he praised Marla Lerieu and had a word for Margaret.

"In our time we have seen many Margarets, and Drina Adams certainly makes her lively and appealing as well as pathetic. One hardened critic, at any rate, was moved by that well-known cry: 'Daddy, I don't want to be a might-have-been!"

"Bless him!" said Drina, and turned to another newspaper, which took the line that Barrie was a wonderful relief after a too long continued diet of obscure and depressing modern plays.

"Here we have genuine sentiment and some genuine humour; a good many sly digs at character traits and development. 'The fault, dear Brutus, is not in our stars but in ourselves. . . .' So, in the magic wood, Barrie's characters take the same paths again, with only slight variations. Marla Lerieu, as one would expect, gives a telling performance as Alice Dearth, and Clement Chandos returns briefly to the stage to give us a moving performance as Mr Dearth, especially in the scene in the wood with Margaret. Drina Adams, who appears by permission of the Igor Dominick Ballet School, made Margaret very real in her brief unreality. Miss Adams, at fourteen, shows great ability and much stage sense. I enjoyed her performance immensely."

"Oh!" Drina's eyes were shining as she struggled amongst the many sheets of newsprint. "Nice man!"

But the critic in the next paper disagreed entirely.

"Drina Adams as Margaret is unfortunately too inexperienced to sustain the difficult part." And that was all he had to say about it.

Drina sat hugging her knees, surrounded by papers, facing the knowledge that no two critics will ever say the same thing and that some seem almost to have seen a different play. *"Drina Adams made Margaret very real in her brief unreality." "Drina Adams is unfortunately too inexperienced to sustain the difficult part."* Which was right? Or was it partly that every play, every performance, meant something different to every human being?

Then she found a paper she had overlooked where the critic said:

"Mr Calum Campbell is to be congratulated on his Barrie season at the Queen Elizabeth Theatre. After an excellent Crichton *he now gives us an equally excellent* Dear Brutus. *Each part was well-played, especially Lady Caroline (Lally Devine) and Margaret (Drina Adams). Clement Chandos was well cast as Mr Dearth and the best scene in the play was undoubtedly that between himself and Margaret, his might-have-been daughter. Drina Adams played Margaret with just the right nuance, half-happy, half-sad. Around me, I noticed, were some eyes that were not quite dry. Quite an achievement with a first-night audience in the West End."*

So, on the whole, Drina was pleased and even elated and she set off cheerfully for the Dominick, meeting Ilonka in Kingsway. Ilonka had read some of the comments and was indignant over the unkind one.

"Well, never mind," said Drina. "I suppose it might be worse. But I'm afraid Queenie will only have read that one. Why do I mind so much what that wretched girl says?"

Daphne, too, had read the unkind criticism and was loudly commenting on it when Drina and Ilonka entered the cloakroom.

"Of *course* she hasn't the experience! We all know that."

"But one critic says that she made people cry," Meryl pointed out shrilly. "And another – "

"Anyway, I don't know why we're wasting our breath on Drina Adams," Daphne added.

Drina went quietly to her usual corner and began to change. She wished, as usual, that Daphne did not dislike her so much, but more than that she was worried to see that Daphne looked pale and ill. She had not seemed herself for some time; her dancing had not been good lately, and she was certainly growing alarmingly tall. Daphne struck Drina as being very unhappy, and if they had been more friendly she would have tried to find out why. But of course it was no good trying to approach Daphne at all.

However, she could not dwell for long on Daphne's possible troubles, for as soon as she emerged from the cloakroom there were others eager to congratulate her. Igor had read all the papers, it seemed, and remarked that the one disgruntled critic had probably had stomach-ache.

"But perhaps I *was* bad," Drina said.

"Well, perhaps you were, but the others do not seem to think so. No, it must have been his stomach, or a headache, or perhaps that his overdraft at the bank is too large."

"Did your father read them?" Drina asked nervously.

"I read them out to him. Yes, even that unpleasant one. Useless to try and hide it. He will reserve his judgement until he sees for himself, my father."

"I *wish* you weren't all coming!" Drina groaned, and soon afterwards ran almost full tilt into Marianne Volonaise in the corridor that led to the studios. Miss

Volonaise looked preoccupied, but she smiled at Drina.

"Did you enjoy it? I see that most of the critics have treated you very kindly."

"Oh, yes, Madam. In a way I loved it."

"Good!" And Miss Volonaise went on her way, a slim, elegant figure in a pale grey dress.

After that it didn't seem to matter at all what the critics said, or that she would be Margaret again that evening, for Drina was caught up in the hard work of the ballet class and, with one hand on the *barre* and her body moving in the familiar rhythms, wanted nothing else.

She had soon settled down into the routine of school and the evening performance and by Wednesday she had forgotten to be nervous and was enjoying herself thoroughly. But each time she acted Margaret it was a little while before she came back to the real world, so tight a hold did the part get on her.

The audiences were good and there had been a few more notices, most of them rather guardedly enthusiastic. No other critic mentioned Drina's performance, but Lally, Marla Lerieu and Clement Chandos came in for a good deal of praise. Drina was glad for Lally, of whom she was very fond.

On Wednesday Drina had visited "The Golden Zither", and she fell in love with the place at once. The restaurant was not large, but it was very attractive; the kitchen quarters had been modernized by the previous tenant, and upstairs were two floors of small, bright rooms. Leaning out of Ilonka's bedroom window it was just possible to see a little square, with cheerful awnings and an odd suggestion of a village. It seemed very strange that the roaring traffic of Piccadilly and the smartness of Mayfair were so near.

So the first week passed and on Sunday Ilonka and

Drina walked in Regent's Park and then sat on Primrose Hill, with London spread out below.

After their walk they made their way to "The Golden Zither" for tea. The restaurant was not open yet, but would be by the end of next week, and already there were advertisements in newspapers and even one on the escalators at Piccadilly Circus.

Terza was at home for tea and so was Mr Lorencz, and Drina soon forgot to be shy with Ilonka's father. He was learning English rapidly and already looked better in health.

Terza told Drina the latest news about the play that was being made from *Diary of a Dancer* and said emphatically that she would not act in it.

"They'll have to find a real actress. I am a dancer. What about you, Drina?"

Drina stared at her blankly.

"Me?"

"You are an actress. You are dark like me and look foreign. Much smaller and a good deal younger, yes, but perhaps it would not matter."

"But I'm not really an actress," Drina said slowly, staggered by the suggestion. "I'm like you, Terza, or rather I want to be. I only really care about dancing. And – and oh! I never could. It would be a huge part – a wonderful part for some girl."

"Why not a wonderful part for *you*?" Mrs Lorencz asked, looking at the earnest, downbent face of the visitor.

Drina looked up then.

"I couldn't do it. I *am* too small and young and, anyway, it would break my heart. Just reading your book, Terza – " But she could say no more.

Mrs Lorencz said slowly, in her clear and assured English, "If you feel like that, child – and we know you

are a good actress – it seems to me that it *ought* to be you. How do you think the girl who played Anne Frank felt? In some ways that must have been almost unbearable, but it was a deeply moving play, so I'm told."

Drina did not argue, but she could not imagine ever playing such an important part; could not imagine *being* Terza. It was in no way possible, but she felt flattered and astonished that Terza should think of it.

Terza, too, did not pursue the subject, but later, when she, Ilonka and Drina were strolling towards Curzon Street, she said, "Mr Blane – who published my book, you know – has kept on wishing that I would write another book. But I said I could not: it was just a diary, written during great trouble and fear."

"But you ought to write another," Drina said eagerly.

"Now I am wondering. It is very pleasant to have money and, more than that, thoughts of a new book keep coming into my head. I find myself haunted by it. Is it like that to be a writer?"

"I don't know," said Drina truthfully. "I've never met one. Or only you, Terza. Oh, do write it! Do! About the Dominick Company, and getting used to England, and your father coming home and "The Golden Zither".

"And call it *Dancer at the Dominick*," said Ilonka, with a little skip.

"It seems so strange that people are interested in us," Terza said humbly, but she did not say that she wouldn't write the book. And, as usual when she had been with the Lorencz family, Drina went home feeling thoughtful and oddly uplifted. They were all so brave, so ready to accept the new country and to put all their troubles and tragedies behind them. It gave Drina herself a wider perspective and made her own narrow world seem extraordinarily safe in comparison.

So *Dear Brutus* went into its second week, and Drina knew that in the daytime a different cast was rehearsing *Mary Rose*. At least, it was not entirely different, for Lally was to be in the next production and so were one or two other people.

The time seemed to pass very quickly and sometimes regret seized Drina in an unexpected grip. *Dear Brutus* had been created and soon would fade away. It always happened, with a play, but she could not help minding. At any rate she would never forget being Margaret and the pleasure and good companionship of the theatre.

"But I'm definitely going to think of nothing but work," she told her grandmother. "The moment the curtain comes down on Saturday night that's going to be that! For a month I shall work harder than ever before. And then it will be holidays. How quickly this term has gone! It seems no time at all since I came back from Italy and now it's getting towards the end of June."

The holidays looked like being very crowded: for first Drina was going to the farm with Jenny; then Antonia Gardino was coming to London and the Chesters would probably take her touring in the car; and at the beginning of September Drina and her grandparents were going to the Edinburgh Festival, and it would be especially exciting that year, because the Dominick Company was to dance there for a week.

Mrs Chester thought it rather odd of Drina to be so pleased.

"My dear, you can see the Dominick any time. I should have thought you'd prefer to see some other company. You will probably, of course, for we're staying into the third week of the Festival, but still –"

"Sometimes they have a sort of International Ballet Company," Drina said dreamily, "and do only new ballets. That would be interesting, but I love to see the Dominick in new places. I've seen them in London and Liverpool, Milan and Genoa. I shall love to see them in Edinburgh."

When Drina returned from the theatre on Friday evening, travelling by taxi with Miss Thorne, Jenny had already arrived at the flat. She leaped up when Drina appeared and embraced her warmly. As Jenny grew older she seemed to be able to show her feelings more easily.

"Oh, Drina, my dear! *What* a long time since we met! And yet you don't alter. I don't believe you've grown at all."

"Half an inch," Drina said, with dignity. "Oh, Jenny, you do look so grown up! I like that yellow dress and look at your shoes! How do you keep them on?"

"Easily enough," Jenny said airily. "I thought I'd leave my farm boots at home, seeing as how I'm staying with a sophisticated London actress."

"I think it's you who are sophisticated," Drina retorted, and it was true. For she was wearing a simple summer dress, no stockings and sandals, and Jenny had certainly grown and altered. She was fifteen now; a well-built girl who tended to be too fat. But she was so healthy, with such a good complexion and such pretty hair, that she made a very pleasant picture in the bright evening light.

Her appearance might have altered, but she was just the same Jenny, eager to hear all about Drina's experiences and to tell her own news, mainly concerning her visits to the farm. She and Drina talked for so long when they were supposed to have gone to bed that Mrs Chester looked in to protest.

But Drina answered cheerfully; "It's Saturday

tomorrow, don't forget, Granny. We can have a late morning. I don't have to be at the theatre 'till five."

"It seems so odd that you're a West End actress," Jenny said thoughtfully, sitting on Drina's bed in her pyjamas. "I thought at the time that *Argument* was just a solitary occasion, but now – "

"I'm *not* an actress," Drina said. "It'll be over tomorrow. I'm just a junior at the Dominick. And I shall still be a junior for two more years, I suppose. Oh, Jenny, we are growing up, though. I thought so tonight when I saw you looking so smart and old."

"Yes, we are," Jenny said soberly. "But don't let my London clothes worry you. That's Mother. I have to give in to her a little. You know I'm ten times happier in jeans or dungarees and boots."

"How much longer will you stay at school?"

"Oh, probably for another couple of years, at least. Until I can get into an agricultural college. I talked to Father a while ago and told him I'd *got* to go; that it was the only thing I wanted. The others cost a lot, but I don't see why I should be left out. Whatever I did it would cost, even going to a commercial college for a year or so. But I'd get a grant and I can get holiday jobs. There's one thing, though." And her face clouded.

"What?"

"Well, you know both Father and Mother have been looking worried just lately, and about a week ago Mother told me that the business wasn't doing too well. But I suppose it will pick up again. It's a very old established firm. I just *have* to go in for farming. I haven't a hope of buying a farm, but I can work on someone else's."

"On your uncle's, perhaps?"

Jenny's face clouded still further.

"They're talking of giving up in a year or two and

going out to Australia to live with their son. It will just about kill me if they do. Really, life can be worrying!"

"You'll have to marry that farmer."

"What farmer?" Jenny demanded.

"Oh, the farmer you're going to fall in love with."

"I haven't met him yet," Jenny said roundly. "I suppose life just doesn't work out the way one wants it. No, I shall do dairying or specialize in poultry, and forget all about marrying. And now, I suppose, I'd better let you go to sleep or you'll be a Margaret with dark rings under your eyes!" And she went off whistling to her own little room.

Drina lay for some time thinking about life. . . . *Dear Brutus* and her unexpected little tastes of fame. . . . hopes and fears for the future. . . . Jenny, with her sound common sense and deep love of the countryside. It was worrying to know that all was not quite well with the Pilgrims, but Drina felt, with Jenny, that things would probably right themselves.

It was good to have Jenny there the next morning and they spent a happy day, helping Mrs Chester to shop for the weekend and then, in the afternoon, walking by the lake in St James's Park. Jenny loved the park and was amused by the children and the innumerable water-fowl.

They returned to the flat for an early tea before Drina left for the theatre and Jenny said, "I shall look forward to seeing your last performance. I don't like *Dear B.*, but I shall like *you*."

"I suppose you wish it were a play about farming!" Drina teased.

Drina enjoyed the early performance and was not in the least tired by the time the eight-thirty one started. This was the last time, so she must savour it. And it seemed to her that the play had a special magic, that the audience was held even more firmly than it had been before. But, as usual while she was on stage, she gave no thought to all those hundreds of people out beyond the footlights.

As on the first night, she was to stay till the end, and when the time came there were many curtains. Drina took one with Clement Chandos and a big bouquet was handed up to her. Later she saw that the card said:

"*From Ilonka, Igor, Jan and all your friends at the Dominick.*"

"You did very well," said Calum Campbell, meeting her near her dressing-room. "A very capable actress, though you are so young. I don't say I won't call on you again sometime."

Drina looked up at him earnestly.

"Oh, please don't, Mr Campbell!"

"Well, you are an extraordinary young woman! I believe you really mean it. Don't you know that there are hundreds of girls your age who would give anything – ?"

"I do know," Drina said gravely. "And I *love* acting. But I don't want to get to love it any more. I don't want to be led away from dancing."

"You won't be," he said, with certainty. "But it's a pity. And I think you'll find yourself doing some more acting before very long, even if dancing *does* hold your heart."

7

The Tragedy of Daphne

Jenny had to go back to Willerbury on the five o'clock train on the Sunday and Drina saw her off at Paddington. As usual she felt rather sad, but they would meet again on July 28th, which was really not very long to wait.

"Get ready for that muck-spreading!" said Jenny, leaning out of the train. It was an old joke.

"There isn't any in August," Drina retorted.

"Well, you can always muck out the cowsheds or the stables. Or the pigs."

"It's not my idea of fun."

"It's work, not fun." But Jenny's eyes were dancing.

"It's fun to you. You love it, odd as it might seem. You'll be the star pupil at that agricultural college."

"I should think so, after all the years I've already put in! I shall win the Golden Spade at the end of the course."

"Do they award one?"

"Well, you know what I mean. There ought to be a farming Oscar. Take care of yourself and don't get too lost in the Dominick."

Drina waved until the train was out of sight and then walked soberly away towards the tube entrance. She always missed Jenny bitterly, and it was a pity that they could not meet more often. For the first time, perhaps, she seriously considered the consequences to her private life of making dancing her career. Jenny would be in the heart of the country somewhere, and she, if she achieved her ambition, might be anywhere: London, America, Spain, even China or Australia. Ballet companies went all over the world.

"But Jenny and I will always be friends," she told herself, as the train rattled and swayed its way south-east.

The next morning she went back to the Dominick and settled down to work hard. Ordinary school examinations were approaching, so it was as well that she had not slacked during *Dear Brutus*. Also there would be the end of the year medical examinations, which used to make her feel so uneasy. But her earlier delicacy seemed to have gone and she felt extremely well. Surely there was nothing to fear on that score?

In the hall she saw Daphne, who certainly did not look well. She was paler than ever and walked with a slouch. She looked as though she had all the troubles of the world on her shoulders.

During break Drina cornered Meryl, who, while she did not always approve of them, was quite friendly with Queenie and Daphne.

"Look here! What *is* the matter with Daphne? She looks awful!"

Meryl looked round to see if they were likely to be overheard and then said in a low voice, "She's afraid that they're going to chuck her out. When Daphne began to look so awful I asked Queenie, but she told me not to tell anyone. Daphne's been afraid all term but she keeps on hoping."

Drina's heart leaped sickeningly. She was appalled. The spectre that hung over all of them seemed very near.

"But they *can't*! Daphne must be mistaken. Why,

she's been dancing longer than I have. She was at the Selswick School in Willerbury when I was there. And – and she was so promising."

"Well, she isn't promising *now*," Meryl said darkly. "You must have noticed that she isn't dancing well, and she's grown so tall. Seems Miss Volonaise warned her mother at the end of last term. Said they'd see how she went on and make up their minds in time for Daphne to go somewhere else in September."

"S-Somewhere else?"

"An ordinary school, I mean. Daphne apparently came back determined to work like anything and prove them all wrong, but she's growing all the time and she's not a bit attractive. You must have noticed how lumpy she's gone?"

"But – " Drina was remembering the little golden-haired girl who had danced so well and had such an opinion of herself. She had never cared for Daphne, but it had not been her wish that they should be rivals. However, she had got used to the knowledge that they would probably continue to be rivals as long as they were both connected with the Dominick.

She felt utterly winded, utterly dismayed. For *Daphne* to have to face that, when she had always cared so much about dancing! Whenever a similar thing had happened Drina had been filled with horror, but so far none of her close companions had been asked to leave the Dominick School, though there had been tragedies at the end of every year. It was these recurring dismissals that kept them all in a slight state of fear and doubt.

"I don't believe it will happen," she said, but was sobered for the rest of the day. Every time she looked at Daphne her heart leaped with pity and there was a touch of admiration, too, because Daphne had gone doggedly and silently through the term. No wonder she had seemed even more unfriendly and unkind than usual; it probably showed the measure of her unhappiness.

"And I," Drina thought, when she had parted from Ilonka after school, "I've been so lucky. Dancing with the Dominick in Genoa ... being Margaret. Even though I pulled that muscle it wasn't really so awful. It gave me Margaret."

For two weeks Drina thought much about Daphne, watching her anxiously in class and ignoring her occasional jibes. But if Daphne had had any definite news she did not make it general.

If anyone else had noticed that Daphne was in trouble there was no comment. The end of term was always a very busy time, and then there was the excitement of the coming holidays. Many of the girls were flying to very distant homes – even as far as Australia, India and South America. Others were hoping to have wonderful trips. Queenie was going to Spain, Bella home to Italy and then on holiday to Sicily. Meryl's family had hired a cabin cruiser and they were going up the Thames, and Jan Williams was going climbing in the Alps with his father.

To add to the general excitement amongst the girls a piece of news had gradually seeped through the school. A new production of *Casse Noisette* was being taken to the Edinburgh Festival, but everyone had assumed that the role of Little Clara would, as usual, go to a young member of the *corps de ballet*. Not Bettina Moore now, for she had relinquished the role, but someone who looked very young.

"But they say it isn't so," said Jill one day. "They're thinking of having a younger girl. One of *us* – one of the Juniors."

"I don't believe it!" said Queenie.

"But it does seem to be true. Think of going to Edinburgh with the Company! Not that I'd have a hope, nor you either, Queenie. We don't look a bit as Little Clara ought to look and, anyway, I shan't be in England," explained Jill.

"I don't see why not," said Queenie. "After all, I'm Beryl Bertram's daughter. When one's mother was a ballerina - "

"You aren't the sort to look like a sweet little child in a white nightgown. Your hair isn't right, for one thing. It wouldn't make any difference if your mother was *prima ballerina assoluta*, that I'm sure," said Jill.

"If it's true and they're going to audition for the part, I shall go," Queenie insisted. "I shall be back from Spain by August 18th."

Drina had heard the news with some excitement, for she had always loved *Casse Noisette* and had often imagined having the role of Little Clara. But perhaps it wasn't true that those in authority were even considering such a thing.

However, that very afternoon, she met Bettina Moore coming out of the rehearsal rooms. Bettina, who had once made so attractive a Little Clara, had always interested Drina and they had grown friendly in Italy during April. Bettina was nineteen, but still looked very young indeed.

She grinned at Drina.

"Hullo, Margaret! I suppose you miss the excitement? Or have you forgotten all about it in the midst of exams?"

"Forgotten!" Drina said. "We had the maths and geography papers today and the maths one was awful. I never *shall* be much good at figures. In fact, I'm hopeless. Bettina, is it true about Little Clara?"

Bettina raised her fair eyebrows.

"What about her?"

"That the Company is going to take one of the Juniors to Edinburgh?"

"I have heard a murmur about it. Seems they think it would make a change and be nice for one of the kids."

"Oh! Everyone will be mad to go! It's one of the dreams of my life to dance Little Clara. I always envied you so much."

Bettina laughed and said, "I got a lot of notice and it was fun at first. But, as you know, there's practically no dancing and, in winter particularly, it can be absolutely wicked sitting about on the stage all that time in a practically transparent nightgown! I used to get awful colds and it was such a strain having to look eager and interested at every moment. But for a few performances in summer – "

"It just couldn't ever happen to *me*," Drina said sadly. "There are dozens who look more like Little Clara than I do."

"Well, I don't know. You look very young and your hair will fasten back with a ribbon. I should think you might have a chance, particularly as you danced with us in Genoa."

"Actually, I'm going to Edinburgh with my family that week. Oh, but it's no use thinking about it." And Drina turned to join Ilonka, who was waving a few yards away.

The next morning there was a letter from Rose.

"Dear Drina,

"Just think! Soon it will be holidays! How quickly this term has gone. The corn is high in the fields and there are scarlet seas of poppies.

"Did I tell you? Mum has arranged for us all to go and

stay on a farm near Hereford. I shall like that ten times better than going to Margate or somewhere, as we used to. They liked Rye last year and Dad suggested a farm for a change.

"Everyone is very excited here, because it's said that they're going to take a member of the School to dance Little Clara at Edinburgh. Apparently some of us are going to be able to go up to town for the audition. But we don't know yet who will be chosen, and there are such a lot of us. Oh, Drina, I should love, love, love to be chosen, but I know I never shall.

"When are you going to the farm? I shall be home on the 27th, but perhaps we'll meet at the audition before that."

Meanwhile, Drina had something far less pleasant to think about, for the next morning Daphne did not appear at the ballet class, and when they had all changed and trooped upstairs to the classroom she was there already, her shoulders hunched and her mousy hair hanging down to hide her face. The English mistress had not arrived and some of Daphne's friends gathered round her.

"What is it, Daph? Why didn't you come to the class? Have you bust your ankle or something?"

"Leave her alone," said Queenie authoritatively, for once with thoughts for someone besides herself.

"But why?" Jill asked. "I don't understand."

"For heaven's sake shut up and leave her alone!" Queenie ordered fiercely, and for perhaps the very first time Drina found herself being grateful for the high-handed manner.

"Yes, shut up," Daphne said, in a muffled voice. "I can't talk. I'm ill. Leave me alone."

But apparently she wasn't ill (though her face was puffy and her eyes red), for she did her school work as usual. However, she rose before anyone else had time to do so and shot from the room and, watching that

flying figure, so obviously desperately seeking solitude, Drina felt sick. So it had happened! The thing that might happen to any of them.

She felt unlike company herself, and the moment she had finished her milk she escaped to the peculiarly shaped piece of land that was generally called the garden, though there was nothing very garden-like about it. It lay between the main Dominick buildings and some of the studios, which were in a different block.

The sun was hot and others were wandering about or sitting on the steps, but there was no sign of Daphne.

Drina had no intention of looking for Daphne; it was just that she knew of a secluded corner between two walls and partly hidden by a sooty shrub, where it was usually possible to be quiet. And there, huddled on the beaten earth, was Daphne, crying and shaking, obviously lost in despair.

Drina stopped, appalled. She, of all people . . . Daphne would never want *her*. She turned to tiptoe away, but Daphne looked up and her face was not pleasant. Drina was to remember it for years afterwards.

"It *would* be you!" The rather pale eyes were so filled with dislike, as well as with utter misery, that Drina didn't know what to say. Nor could she move. She seemed to be pinned there, close to the uninviting laurel bush.

"I suppose you're *glad*," the hard, bitter voice went on. "You're bound to be. I should have been if it were *you*. I've never liked you. Lucky, lucky little Drina, getting everything and never growing an inch!"

Drina gulped and opened her mouth to say something, but Daphne went on, "I've got to leave and go to an ordinary school. I shall never be a dancer. And

I've never wanted anything else as long as I can remember. I'd sooner die than have to face this. Well, go on – laugh!"

Drina moved two steps into the corner, her hands tightly clasped. She was almost praying for wisdom, for the ability to say the right thing. Comfort Daphne she never could, that was clear. Probably no one on earth could. But somehow she had to stop the hate. . . .

"Daphne, I'm not glad. And I don't believe you would have been if it were me. We're not monsters, and don't you see? It brings it – the same possibility – nearer all of us."

Daphne gave an ugly laugh.

"That's likely, isn't it? *You* danced the changeling, *you* danced in Genoa with the Dominick, *you* get wonderful chances to act in the West End. You get everything. You're rich and good-looking and spoilt – "

"Oh, Daphne!"

"Well, you are. Miss Volonaise notices you, and young Igor admires you. . . . You can do no wrong. Well, I *hate* you!" All her bitterness and despair had quite clearly gone into her concentrated dislike of the girl before her.

"I wish you didn't," Drina said. Her throat felt tight and her legs were shaking. "If only there was something I could say. It's terrible for you. . . . I should want to die, too, if it happened to me."

"Well, it won't. You needn't worry. Oh, go away and leave me."

"There's the bell!" Drina said wretchedly.

"It won't worry me. I'm going home. Miss Volonaise said I could if I liked. But I'll have to stick out the rest of the term, so you'll be able to gloat."

Sorrow and pity began to give place to temper. Drina felt her colour rising and her eyes flashed.

"Oh, Daphne, don't be such an idiot! Take it out on me if it helps, but don't think that I shall gloat. How could I? I'm not a beast, and I'm not selfish or spoilt. I hope not, anyway. You can remember that I *mind*. I mind dreadfully. And if you weren't such a blind idiot you'd see that I do." And then she shot away, catching up with the anxious Ilonka on the steps.

Ilonka had been looking for her.

"Drina, you'll be late for class. What's the matter?"

"Daphne," Drina said breathlessly. "Oh, Ilonka, it's awful! She's got to leave the Dominick, and I found her crying. She hates me. She thinks I'm gloating, but really I'd give anything in the world for it not to have happened to her."

"She is not the only one to go," Ilonka remarked, as they hurried upstairs. "There are a lot more, but mostly in the top class. They heard that they are not to be Senior students. Three of them were crying in the cloakroom."

"Mostly," Drina said soberly, with her hand on the classroom door, "I think we're lucky to know exactly what we want from life, but just now I'm not so sure. What happens when it's all taken away? Daphne says she'd sooner die and I think she means it. I should."

"But one has to go on living," said Ilonka, who had lost her country and all her old friends.

Drina was very grave and withdrawn for the rest of the day, haunted by the memory of Daphne's face and voice. Daphne would clearly never forgive her for her own good fortune; that was understandable, perhaps, but hard to accept. Drina supposed gloomily that it was never easy to accept immovable dislike.

But worst of all was the memory of Daphne's own despair.

8

Little Clara

Because of the tragedy of Daphne, Drina had almost forgotten about *Casse Noisette* and it was a considerable shock when Mr Dominick and Miss Volonaise came to watch the ballet class one morning a week before the end of term.

"As you may have heard," Miss Volonaise said to the assembled girls, most of them arrested in their preliminary exercises at the *barre*, "we are thinking of having a student to dance Little Clara in the production of *Casse Noisette* we are taking to Edinburgh at the end of August. Now, for obvious reasons it can't be anyone who will be away then. I know that many of you are travelling long distances, for one reason or another. Put up your hands, all those girls who will find it quite impossible to be in London during the last ten days or so in August, and Edinburgh for the first week in September."

A great many reluctant hands went up. There were only half a dozen who would not be away: Drina, Ilonka, Queenie, Lorna and two others.

Miss Volonaise nodded.

"I see. Well, we have already chosen half a dozen girls from lower classes. We propose to hold an audition tomorrow afternoon. Now carry on with the class, please." And she smiled at the teacher.

Drina was at first stiff with excitement and anxiety

but, as usually happened, she soon forgot everything but the familiar movements. Besides, Miss Volonaise must really know already whom she would choose. The audition was probably only a matter of form. But oh! to dance Little Clara! To take a curtain with Catherine Colby and Peter Bernoise, as Bettina used to do!

Finally they were stopped and Miss Volonaise turned from Mr Dominick to say, "Drina and Lorna, would you like to come to the audition?"

Queenie gave a small cry of protest, hastily stifled, and Marianne Volonaise looked at her quickly.

"I'm sorry, Queenie, but you just don't look like our idea of Little Clara. By the way, there will also be half a dozen girls from Chalk Green. They have to have their chance, too, you know. And we shall need to choose two. There must be an understudy."

Daphne, who had dropped her ballet classes, said bitterly when she heard the news, "Drina again! I might have known!" Since the day when she had cried and gone home she had been hard and cold, not even seeming to want the company of her friends.

"Yes, Drina *again*," Queenie agreed.

"And Lorna," Drina pointed out. She had been for a while elated, but now the pleasure had gone.

However, by the time she went home she was eager again, daring to dream of the possibility of being chosen. In Genoa she had thought that she would never dance with the Dominick again until she was nearly grown-up, perhaps never. But to go with them to Edinburgh at Festival time! To be *part* of the Festival – a real dancer!

"If only, if *only* it could happen!" she said to her grandmother, who, as usual, was rather dismayed. She had hoped to have a proper holiday without thoughts of Drina's career.

"I think you do enough. You ought to have a real holiday."

"But I shall get one, in any case. The farm with Jenny, then the time with Antonia. Oh, Granny, *think* if I could be Little Clara!"

Mrs Chester thought and did not like the idea at all. Betsy had danced Little Clara when she was just sixteen and it was then that the critics had begun to say that here, perhaps, was a future ballerina. Not that they could really tell, when Little Clara only had one short dance in the first act and, in some productions, a few steps in the last one. But Betsy had been a delightful Little Clara, looking years younger than her age, and that indefinable quality of personality had come through strongly.

Drina was just the same. Her grandmother saw her again as she had been after *The Changeling*, standing before the blue curtain at the Dominick, curtseying and smiling, holding a bouquet. It sometimes seemed to her very bitter that it was all, probably, to be gone through again; after all, it had started already.

She sighed, remembering that Betsy had never had much time for a private life. Even her marriage had been, to Mrs Chester's mind, unsatisfactory, though Betsy and her Italian husband had seemed very much in love. Drina, from a couple of months after her birth, had been in the care of a nanny and not very much later Betsy was flying off to distant countries. Even when at home she had been constantly in the limelight, pursued by the press, always busy, noticed everywhere she went.

"I would have liked you to have an ordinary life," Mrs Chester said, speaking her thoughts aloud, as she rarely did.

Drina ran to hug her, an unusual gesture, for they

were hardly ever demonstrative.

"Oh, Granny! But I can't imagine an ordinary life now."

"I don't suppose you can," Mrs Chester agreed heavily. "Anyway, you may not be chosen."

When Drina and Lorna went shyly into the Dominick rehearsal rooms the next afternoon they found the six from Chalk Green already there, standing in a tense bunch near the piano. A second later Drina spied Rose and, forgetting nervousness, she dashed down the room to her friend.

"Oh, *Rose*! How lovely to see you! I'm so glad you were chosen!"

"This far but no further," said Rose. "What an age it seems since that day you pulled your muscle. I haven't seen you since we came to *Dear Brutus*. And then you were Margaret, not yourself."

"But in some ways this term has simply flown."

They stood talking until Miss Volonaise, Igor Dominick, the Company ballet-mistress and the pianist arrived, and then an uneasy silence fell. It was an important moment.

They each had to do a very simple dance and then Miss Volonaise said, "We'd like to see some of you in costume. Drina Adams, Rose Conway, Clarice Paul, June Marlow . . . run along and find the wardrobe-mistress. She's somewhere about, probably in my office. She has nightgowns and hair-ribbons for you. Never mind about the dress for the party."

The nightgowns were very soft and full, falling from gathered shoulders. Drina slipped into hers, fumbling a little because her fingers felt stiff. Then she combed her hair and tied it back with a blue ribbon.

"Oh, Rose, I'm scared!"

"Mine's too long," said Rose. "I shall probably fall

flat on my face."

But she didn't. She looked a very charming Little Clara.

"It'll be you," said Drina presently, and tried to keep the envy out of her voice. After all, *she* had had all the luck so far and a trip to Edinburgh would be a wonderful experience for Rose.

"No, you! You're far more experienced."

In the end Miss Volonaise, after a long consultation with Igor Dominick and the ballet-mistress, turned to them, smiling.

"We have decided to take Drina to Edinburgh as Little Clara, and Rose is to go also, as understudy."

Quite forgetting, in the excitement of the moment, that they were in the presence of the great ones, Drina and Rose embraced each other wildly, their hair flying out behind. Rose's ribbon fell off and hung on her nose and Igor Dominick laughed.

"It's more than the pair of you deserve. Been watching any rehearsals lately?" He had once, long ago, caught the two of them on a flat roof, looking down into that very room, watching the Company rehearsing a new ballet.

"No, Mr Dominick," said Drina, grinning. "We're very good now."

"I should hope so. Well, we'll let you both know the date and time of the first rehearsal. It will only mean a certain amount of work, as the ballet's been in the repertoire very recently. But there are new sets and a few new ideas. What about accommodation in Edinburgh?"

"I was going anyway," Drina explained. "We're staying at the Highland Hotel in Princes Street."

"Good enough! And Rose?"

"Bed and breakfast, I suppose, Mr Dominick," said

Rose.

"Could your mother go with you? You'll have to have someone. You'll be much the youngest. Not fifteen yet, are you?"

"No. Not till the winter."

"Well, don't worry, we'll fix something. And don't forget to behave yourselves."

"He's nice!" Rose said breathlessly, as they changed out of the nightgowns.

"Yes," Drina agreed. She was very, very happy to know that yet another dream was coming true, but she felt a little worried about Rose. It seemed so dull just to be the understudy, though it would be wonderful to be in Edinburgh together.

But Rose soon put her fears at rest.

"I don't care a bit. I'd *sooner* understudy you. I shall be there and part of it all without having to worry too much. And I shall get paid. That will thrill Mum no end. Though I don't know what she'll say about having to have someone with me."

Drina, however, had another plan, and she expounded it to her grandmother soon after she had told the exciting news.

"Oh, Granny, couldn't she stay with *us*? You know you said you had to book a double room for me because there were no single ones left?"

"Her money certainly wouldn't cover the Highland Hotel," said Mrs Chester. "It's one of the most expensive in Edinburgh." But when she saw Drina's expression her face softened. "Oh, very well, you may invite her. It will be nice for you to have a companion and Rose is really a very nice, well-mannered girl. As you say, we're having to pay for your double room, and it won't cost so very much more."

"Oh, Granny, thank you! But what about the theatre?

We'll have to have a chaperone. Isn't it a bore?"

Mrs Chester laughed very ruefully.

"How many times are they giving the ballet?"

"On the Monday night, and on Wednesday afternoon, Thursday evening, Saturday afternoon, and Saturday evening. Each time with the new Igor Dominick ballet, *Sea Green Maiden.*"

"Five times? Well, don't worry about it. I suppose I can come with you. It won't be the first time I've spent hours backstage."

Drina looked at the calm face of her grandmother, knowing full well what the offer entailed.

"It's terribly nice of you, because you won't enjoy it a bit, will you? And I'm sure Rose's mother wouldn't be able to leave the family to go with her."

Later that evening she telephoned Rose at Chalk Green to tell her the plans, and Rose was thrilled.

"Oh, Drina! I've never stayed in a hotel!"

"Really never?" Drina had forgotten how few experiences Rose had had. Her parents were not well-off and she had had few opportunities to travel.

"No. Only in seaside boarding-houses and that little guest-house at Rye. And the Highland is a really big hotel, isn't it?"

"Huge, I believe. And Igor says he's staying there with his father. Miss Volonaise, too, perhaps."

"Good gracious!" said Rose frankly. "I shall use the staff entrance!"

"Don't be an idiot! We may never see them. There'll be *hundreds* of people."

"Anyway, it's wonderful of your grandparents. Everything's wonderful!"

"Even Christine?"

"Oh, her!" exclaimed Rose. "She's going to Sweden; we never hear the end of it. And, thank heaven, you'll

have her next term instead of us. Oh, here's Emilia –"
the telephone was in a rather public place, at the end of
a corridor. A moment later Rose turned back to say –
"she sends her love."

"Send her mine and tell her to think of me when she's
in Genoa. Good-bye!"

"Good-bye and thank you very, very much." And
Rose rang off.

So the last week of the summer term passed and
Drina mostly enjoyed it, though she hated to see
Daphne's hard and sullen face and was unhappy when
Queenie, and Daphne also, made unkind comments
about the choice for *Casse Noisette*.

"Oh, shut up!" Ilonka said on one occasion. "Drina
was chosen because she was the most suitable – you
know that, really. Why must you be so unkind?"

"Why must Drina be so lucky?" Queenie asked
nastily.

"Women!" Jan Williams remarked, overhearing. "For
heaven's sake leave the girl alone. I never knew a
worse cattery." And he took Drina by the arm and
marched her away, saying, "Don't listen to them.
They're jealous. And you'll make a fantastic Little
Clara."

Finally came breaking-up day and Drina's heart
ached for Daphne as she watched her collect her things
and walk through the hall for the last time.

Drina and Rose had just one afternoon together and
they went up the river to Greenwich. Both enjoyed
themselves and Drina revelled as usual in the London
scene. But she was looking forward greatly to being in
the country, for her months at Chalk Green had made
her long sometimes for clearer air and the sweet smells
of fields and woods.

The next day, with just a small suitcase, she caught the Willerbury train and, as it sped past the crowding buildings of London, she settled down to review the term. It had been good on the whole, in spite of her trouble with the leg muscle, and some things had been unforgettable, especially the run of *Dear Brutus* and being chosen to dance Little Clara.

At the thought of the Edinburgh Festival her heart lifted with excitement and a touch of panic. But first would come the time with Jenny and then Antonia's visit.

As the fields began she sat there happily, looking forward to the immediate future.

BOOK TWO
Ballet in Edinburgh

1
Holidays

On the station platform at Willerbury stood Jenny, Mark Playford and Joy Kelly. Joy, like Mark, had once gone to the Selswick School and still had ballet lessons from the two women who had taken over the school.

"We met Jenny and said we'd come with her to meet you," Mark explained, seizing Drina's case.

"Mother had to go to a meeting," Jenny said quickly. "Something to do with her precious Guild. So I said we'd get the bus if you hadn't much luggage, or a taxi if necessary. But first come and have something in the refreshment room – then we can talk."

Joy eyed Drina with some awe as they all walked along the platform.

"You don't look much different, and you certainly don't look a day more than twelve."

"It's very trying," Drina said, grinning. "I must say I'm getting tired of it. Granny won't let me wear high heels and older sort of clothes."

"But why *should* she look different?" Jenny asked, as they crowded round a table and Mark ordered coke for four.

"Oh, I don't know. She's so terribly important, isn't she? Acting in West End plays and now going to dance Little Clara at the Edinburgh Festival." Joy longed to make ballet her career, but knew that she had almost no chance of it. The most she could hope for, to liven up her spare time when she got a job, would be to dance in charity shows and perhaps in the Willerbury Christmas pantomime.

"If you saw me at the Dominick," said Drina cheerfully, "you'd realize that I'm just a junior and going to remain so for two more years. Then, with luck, we go up into the Senior School and get chances to walk on and so on."

"To *walk on*? But you've done far more than that already! Jenny showed me the Genoa cuttings when you posted them to her, with the translations. You danced with the Dominick. A *real* dance and got mentioned in the papers."

"It was only sheer luck!" Drina assured her. "And Clara is sheer luck, too, because I'm small and look young and they want to try a junior."

"You always were too modest," Jenny said indignantly. "I know you mean it, but it's rubbish. You've got something and they know it. Will Mark be in your class?"

"Probably not," said Drina. "He's a few months older, after all. We share lessons with the boys, but not ballet classes. Are you still half-dreading it, Mark?"

Mark laughed. "I've said good-bye to my school here and am all set to be a ballet dancer. No, I want it, and I can stand the teasing. But it's time that the average British male stopped thinking of ballet dancing as sissy. After all it's very energetic. I think I read somewhere that during the last war Russian dancers got double rations, like men who did heavy work. It may not be true, but I tell anyone who laughs!"

"When you're partnering Drina at the Dominick or Covent Garden," said Jenny, "they'll sing a different tune. Probably they'll be begging you to get them tickets for gala performances, so that they can take their wives or girlfriends. I shouldn't worry what they say."

"I don't," said Mark. "But there's no doubt that it's a big step."

"And now you're just on the point of going off to Italy. Isn't he lucky, Drina? He's going to Rome with his uncle and aunt."

"Oh, I do so long to see Rome!" Drina cried.

"Well, you didn't do so badly," Jenny said roundly. "You saw Milan and Como and Genoa; and all those lovely places along the Riviera."

"It seems like a dream now."

"I bet it does, now that you're back in grim old Willerbury," Joy remarked. It was her dream to live in London, where there might be almost constant performances of ballet and she could queue in Floral Street for the cheapest seats at the Royal Opera House. "But look here! Tell us about Daphne. Jenny says she's left the Dominick."

Immediately Drina looked grave and some of her cheerfulness fell away from her.

"It's true. She *has* left. I felt terrible about it."

"Why? She never liked you and didn't trouble to hide it," Joy said bluntly, and Drina flushed.

"I can't help it. Perhaps it is silly of me, but it's not all minding about Daphne – though I did care – it's that it might so easily be any of us. It's always dreadful to watch. She grew too tall and her dancing went off, however hard she tried. She's going to the Pakington School not far from Buckingham Palace, where I went for one term."

"It is hard," Mark said. "She was such a promising kid. So pretty with that golden hair, and a good dancer."

"That's what I mean," Drina pointed out. "There sometimes comes a point where people who showed promise suddenly and inexplicably go downhill. They haven't the physique, or they grow tall, or they just never will have the technique. That's why we all keep our fingers crossed. I don't know how Daphne will exist. She does mind so much."

"She'll take up something else, I suppose," Jenny said. "But it *must* be awful. If it were me and farming – "

"Oh, we all know you're only happy in a cowshed," Joy teased. "Oh, well, I must go. Nice to see you, Drina. I shall look out for bits about you in the papers during the Festival."

Joy and Mark went off and Drina reached for her case, snapped it open and handed Jenny a ballet magazine.

"I didn't want to show them. It looks too like showing off. But it's nice, isn't it?" On the cover was an enlargement of the photograph that Igor had taken on Isola Bella.

Jenny gaped at it.

"The same one that was in the London *Standard*." Oh, Drina! It looks wonderful! On the cover, too. When did you get it?"

"Igor brought it round yesterday evening. I don't take the magazine. He's really pleased and he's going to make me share the money, if he gets paid – and he ought to get quite a lot."

"You must show Mother. It will cheer her up. She still seems very worried, and I don't know what to do about it. She'll rush out and order half a dozen copies. Is there a caption?"

"It's inside the cover. *'Young Girl by a Fountain. Miss Drina Adams, of the Dominick Ballet School, on holiday in Italy. Taken by Igor Dominick, Junior.'* "

"Well, I never! I do call that fame. When I get my photo in *The Farmers' Weekly* I'll send *you* a copy." And Jenny seized Drina's suitcase and led the way to the bus-stop near the station.

Mrs Pilgrim had just reached home when they opened the gate and she greeted Drina warmly. But Drina was immediately struck by the fact that she looked older; her hair had gone very grey.

"Well, here's the famous visitor! What a long time since I saw you, my dear. Last September, wasn't it? You look very well and very pretty."

Drina blushed and Jenny laughed.

"She does look pretty. It's having more colour, partly. Italy gave her a gorgeous tan and she's never lost it."

Mrs Pilgrim looked thoughtfully at the visitor, remembering a day during their long holiday in Wales, when Drina had poured out her heart about her hopes and fears for the future. So far all had gone very well and she earnestly hoped that things would continue to go well for Drina. The tragedy of Daphne Daniety must not be repeated here. But at the moment there seemed little chance of it.

Drina had not grown much, but she had certainly developed mentally, and Mrs Pilgrim found herself, during that evening, treating her almost as an adult. Jenny had always seemed old for her age and now Drina seemed to have caught up, though she was actually a few months younger.

"Well, I hope you enjoy the farm," Mrs Pilgrim said, a trifle doubtfully as the girls went off to bed. "It'll be a great change from West End theatres and the Dominick Ballet School."

"I love the country now," said Drina. "I'm looking forward to it, *and* to seeing Esmeralda."

The next morning at eleven o'clock, Mrs Pilgrim

drove both girls out into the Warwickshire fields and deposited them at the farm. She was not even staying for lunch, as all the boys, except Philip, were home.

"Have a good time. Don't do anything rash. I'll collect you a week tomorrow, Drina, and put you on the train in Willerbury."

Jenny's uncle and aunt gave the girls a wonderful welcome and then they went up into the room they always shared; a room with uneven floorboards, thick oak beams and a window in a gable. All round the farm the cornfields rolled in pale gold beauty, shining faintly in the sun. The apples were turning red on the trees in the old orchard, and Esmeralda lay in the grass, his eyes on an unsuspecting bird. He was an elegant grey cat, very big and strong, and Drina loved him, though she saw him so little.

"But I wish he wouldn't hunt. Shall I clap my hands, Jenny? That poor bird!"

"He won't bother," said Jenny, joining her at the window. "The sun's too hot and he's really feeling lazy. There! He's rolled over. Merry!"

Esmeralda sat up, stretched and advanced slowly towards the grass below the gable window. Then he leaped into the big old pear-tree that grew close to the wall and climbed rapidly upwards. Drina leaned out and seized him when he was near enough.

"Oh, you clever thing! More graceful than any ballet dancer. And just right when you're called after a ballet. I suppose you've forgotten me?"

But Esmeralda did not seem to have done. He purred and stayed contentedly in Drina's arms, while Jenny began her usual rapid and untidy unpacking.

Then she scrambled into her oldest blouse and jeans, fastened her sandals and announced that she was ready.

"Do hurry up, Drina. I'll go on. I'll see you in the yard."

So began a happy week. The weather was good and Drina revelled in the sweet air, the bright splashes of poppies and sometimes, but very rarely, of cornflowers, the green twilight of the woods, and the beauty of the remote Warwickshire villages, with their brick and timber houses, their orchards and flowery gardens. Sometimes there was a big house dreaming in parkland, and these old and lovely buildings always gave Drina special delight.

The Warwickshire countryside was by no means as dear to her as the satisfying curves of the Chiltern Hills, but she liked it, and also places like Warwick, with its castle and ancient streets, and Stratford, with the River Avon and the great Memorial Theatre.

They helped on the farm in the mornings and in the afternoons and early evenings walked or cycled far afield, and gradually life at the Dominick seemed very remote and the coming experiences in Edinburgh so far in the future that they scarcely seemed possible.

"Dance for me!" Jenny said one day, as they sat in the poppies and marguerites at the side of a cornfield. "I seem to remember another day, a long time ago, when we talked in a cornfield and I said I was Gipsy Jenny and was sure you'd be a dancer."

And Drina laughed and tucked some poppies into her hair, then she took two brilliant scarlet ones, one in each hand, and began to dance on the cleared space at the side of the field. Tomorrow the combine harvester would come in and the tall golden oats would be cut.

She kept her sandals on, since the ground was prickly, and she danced very lightly and gracefully, humming to herself. The poppy petals fell as she moved.

"What was that?" Jenny asked, as her friend returned to her side.

"A bit of the Rose Adagio, but it's hopeless in sandals."

"The Poppy Adagio, I should think. Oh, I am going to be proud of you one day!"

"I hope so," Drina said soberly. "But don't count on it. Better not."

They cycled on and by some mistake found themselves lost and it was getting towards supper-time. They had forgotten to take the map and, unless Drina was with her, Jenny never went far from the farm.

"We shouldn't have come so far," she said ruefully. "That last signpost must have been wrong. Someone has moved it round or something. And now we seem to be going in the wrong direction. There's not even a farm to ask at."

"And I think my tyre's gone flat," Drina announced.

"Oh, *no*! I'm so hungry I could eat a horse. Let me pump it for you."

Jenny pumped, but the tyre remained obstinately flat and air could be heard hissing out through what seemed a large gash.

"You've given it a terrible rip! That'll take some mending. Have you got any money?"

"Only two pence. I spent it all on those ices in Warwick," Drina remarked.

"And I've got about nine pence. So we can't pay a garage if there should happen to be one, which looks highly unlikely, *or* have something to eat if we find a café. Can you ride at all?"

"There'll be no tyre left if I do," said Drina.

Suddenly they both felt hot, grubby and rather tired, as well as hungry. They had had a long day and the dreaming golden-green countryside seemed to offer no solution. They saw a roofline and thought it was a farm, but it turned out to be only a barn, with no dwelling in sight.

"Like the Sahara," said Jenny, looking ruefully at a peppermint she had found in a corner of her pocket.

Suddenly there was a loud hooting and a lorry drew up beside them. A red-haired young man of about nineteen looked out at them enquiringly. He seemed amused.

"Anything I can do for you? You seem to have a flat!"

"The tyre's ripped," said Jenny. "We can mend ordinary punctures, but this seems to have gone a bit far, and we're tired and hungry." She went on to explain rapidly that they were not sure of their road and told where they were staying.

The young man immediately looked interested, but still rather amused by their plight, and Jenny was obviously slightly on her guard.

"Pilgrims' Farm. But that's the next one to us. Hop in and I'll take you back in no time. Well, in twenty minutes or so. Don't you know this country?"

"Pretty well," Jenny said. "But we must be all of ten miles from the farm and we forgot the map. This is such a tangle of lanes. But how can you live at the next farm? That's Hogdens'."

"I know," he said patiently. "I live there now. Been there for a week and, as a matter of fact, I used to live round here when I was young. I'm Robert Hogden. I'll stick the bikes in the back."

"Oh!" said Jenny. "My aunt did say something about your having arrived. But I never expected – " She was going to say that she had not expected brilliantly red hair and anything but a country voice and manner, but obviously that wouldn't be tactful.

"Sorry if I'm a disappointment, kid," he said, with something of the indulgence he might have brought to a younger sister, and Jenny, who rarely felt annoyance, flushed.

"My name is Jenny Pilgrim and I'm fifteen. If you'll really take us back it's very kind of you. We shall be most grateful, shan't we, Drina?"

"Oh, yes," said Drina.

They both crowded into the seat beside the driver and the lorry started on its way. Robert Hogden occasionally glanced at them sideways, his face still a trifle amused, though in many ways it was a surprisingly mature face for so young a man. Jenny remembered that he had lost his parents suddenly and felt sorry for him, but it had annoyed her to sense condescension in his voice and look. He talked to them as though they were very young, asking politely about their schools and hobbies.

"Thank you *very* much, Mr Hogden," Jenny said when they reached the farm and their bicycles were lifted out of the lorry. "It was very kind of you."

"Don't mention it," he said. "Be seeing you again, I expect. Don't forget the map next time."

"Hum!" said Jenny thoughtfully, as they took their bicycles to the shed.

"Why 'hum'? Didn't you like him? I thought you were a bit stiff."

"Oh, he's quite good-looking and seems pleasant, but he thought we were kids. I'm getting to the stage when I hate that. It's so silly, when I'm so huge."

Drina laughed, "Well, I suppose we are kids to him."

"Oh, rubbish! He's only about nineteen. I shall soon catch up."

"Catch up and marry him," Drina said, without thinking, and saw Jenny flush most unusually.

"Don't be an idiot!" she said, very shortly for her. "I don't marry people just because they spring up on the next farm."

"No, but you want to marry a farmer. I only meant it would be nice if you were to fall in love with him in a year or two."

"Oh – *nice!*" said Jenny. "But life isn't like that. I don't say it wouldn't be convenient and all that. It's a good farm and the Hogdens are very old. I suppose it'll be Robert's one day. But I bet he's got a girlfriend already; a willowy little thing, with curls and baby blue eyes."

"Then she won't be much use as a farmer's wife."

"She'll probably take over the poultry or something," said Jenny. "Something light. Though heaven knows you can't call cleaning out ducks particularly light work! I expect she's called Maisie."

"But why?"

"It just came. Oh, never mind red-headed Robert! Let's go and see what there is to eat. I'm simply folding up with hunger." And they ran, laughing, towards the back door.

2
To Edinburgh

Mrs Pilgrim arrived at the end of the week as she had promised and Drina said a rather sad good-bye to Jenny, as well as to Esmeralda and Jenny's uncle and aunt. It would probably be a long time before she saw them all again.

Mrs Pilgrim drove her back to Willerbury and put her into the London train, with some magazines and a small box of chocolates.

"I wish I could see your Little Clara in Edinburgh. I always feel I've got a share in you."

"Oh, you have!" Drina said warmly. "It was you who gave me the prospectus for the Selswick School and took me to my very first ballet. Only four or five years ago, but it seems such an age."

For the first half-hour or so of the journey Drina sat and worried about the Pilgrims. According to Jenny both her parents were still worried, and Drina had seen for herself that Mrs Pilgrim looked far from her old self. The firm of Pilgrim, Watkin and Moore had been doing badly for some time and so far things had not righted themselves.

Mr Chester was at Paddington to meet her, having just started his holidays from the office, and Drina chattered away as they drove to Westminster, telling all about the happenings at the farm.

"And tomorrow there's Antonia," she said

contentedly. "I did like her so much and it will be fun to show her England. I'm so glad that there's ballet at Covent Garden *and* at the Festival Hall. She loves it so."

The Chesters had never met Drina's Italian cousin, whom Drina herself had only met for the first time in the spring, but they were quite looking forward to her visit. Mrs Chester enjoyed having visitors and was, though she would never have admitted it, a little curious about Drina's Italian relations. This was a considerable change of attitude, as she had spent a number of years trying to ignore their existence.

All three went to Victoria the following evening and Drina was very impatient for the boat-train to arrive.

"I wonder if she had a good journey? I hope she wasn't sick. The papers said, 'Channel moderate to rough'." It had been a grey, windy day, but now the sun was shining and the forecast was more hopeful.

The train arrived and people began to pour out on to the platform. It was a little time before Drina spied her cousin, but at last she picked out the tall, slim figure of Antonia Gardino. Antonia was fifteen and a half; very pretty and well-dressed.

She came up to them with two middle-aged Italian ladies, who had been her escort from Genoa, and introductions took place. But the Italians were anxious to get to their hotel adjoining the station and very soon the Chesters, Drina and Antonia were driving along Victoria Street.

"It's lovely to see you again!" said Drina, and Antonia said rather shyly, in her slightly stilted English, "It is lovely to see you, Drina. How long it seems since that evening when you left Genoa. And now I see London."

Her eyes were very busy as they approached the Abbey, bathed in brilliant evening light, and Drina tried to see it all as the stranger was seeing it.

"That's Big Ben, of course, and the Houses of Parliament. Whitehall up there, and that's Westminster Bridge."

"Antonia will be tired, Drina," said Mrs Chester. "She won't want to bother now."

But Antonia did not seem tired.

"It all looks so wonderful," she said, and later exclaimed at the view from her window.

"Oh, it's so exciting to be here!" she said in Italian. "I've been simply living for it. Have you forgotten all your Italian, Drina?"

"Oh, no," said Drina, in the same language. "We'll speak it when we're alone. It will be good practice for me."

"And we're going to the ballet?"

"Yes. To Covent Garden so see *Lac des Cygnes* and to the Royal Festival Hall to see *Graduation Ball, Symphony for Fun* and *Witch Boy. Witch Boy's* very modern, but most exciting. I've seen it once. It *will* be fun to show you everything!"

And it was fun, as well as very satisfying, for Antonia was receptive and intelligent, eager to get to know and understand the new country.

Together they went about London; up and down the river by boat, to the Tower, St Paul's, Hampstead Heath, the Zoo, the parks. The weather was sunny for the most part and sometimes very hot indeed. On the Saturday afternoon, when they went with Mr and Mrs Chester to the Festival Hall, the heat was intense and the flower-beds by the river blazed with colour.

Antonia was deeply impressed by the Festival Hall; by the entrance hall, the wide staircases, and the roof-gardens, from which they could look up and down the river. They sat in the front row of the Grand Tier, with the boxes jutting out on either side between them and the stage.

"It's a marvellous building," Drina said thoughtfully, when they had studied their programmes. "I love it for concerts, but I never think it has much atmosphere for ballet. Nothing like so much as Covent Garden or the Dominick."

But Drina enjoyed the ballet all the same, soon growing quite lost in the world before her and forgetting the bright scenes out of doors. *Witch Boy*, as it had done on the first occasion some time before, whipped her up into a great state of tension and excitement; it was a very strange ballet and almost frightening in parts, especially when the Witch Boy was hanged and his vast shadow moved against the backcloth.

Graduation Ball had always delighted her, especially the antics of the naughtiest girl and the *pas de deux* that really belonged to the ballet *La Sylphide* that she had never seen. *Symphony for Fun* was another very modern ballet, but Drina had by then learned to enjoy modern music and movement. Not, certainly, in the lost and enchanted state of mind that she usually brought to the great classical works, but they made a change and were stimulating.

"All the same, wait until you see *Swan Lake* at Covent Garden," Drina said to Antonia, as, still rather dazed, they made their way out into the hot sunshine again.

For the visit to the Royal Opera House Drina wore the scarlet dress that had been bought for her in Italy and Antonia looked almost grown up in a full green dress and a little silver cape. The visitor drew a long breath as the taxi stopped outside the Opera House.

"The Royal Opera House, Covent Garden!" she murmured. "And I am here. So often have I read of it."

"I used to feel like that," Drina agreed. "Every time I came it seemed like a miracle. But now it's a sort of second home." She followed her grandmother up the short flight of stairs to the Stalls Circle and then said dramatically: "Antonia, look!"

And Antonia looked, standing stock still in everyone's way.

"Oh, Drina! It's a little like La Scala, isn't it? All those tiers and tiers of seats." And people, hearing the eager Italian, smiled and moved round her.

Perhaps because she was with Antonia there seemed to be a special enchantment about that evening. Drina had seen *Le Lac des Cygnes* a number of times, but it could never grow stale for her. She especially loved parts of the second act, though she had for some reason never liked the dance of the cygnets, and the third act – the ball scene – was always perfect. Watching the Black Swan *pas de deux* she found herself dreaming of the day when she might be a great ballerina, with the same flashing technique of the dancer on the stage before her.

"I don't think I ever enjoyed anything so much before," said Antonia with a sigh, as they emerged into the warm, darkening streets and walked towards the Strand in search of a taxi.

"It was very enjoyable," Mrs Chester admitted. "Odette-Odile was one of Betsy's favourite roles." She now often spoke of her daughter's career, though for many years Drina had not even known that her mother had been a great ballerina.

"The great Elizabeth Ivory!" said Antonia.

"But do remember not to say anything to people," Drina begged. "It's all right to Rose, as I told you, and Miss Whiteway, but not to anyone else."

Rose had met the Italian cousin by this time and had

accompanied them on one or two trips round London, for she had returned from Herefordshire a few days before. She had come back looking suntanned and well, but confessed to Drina that her home seemed very hot and stuffy. The little rooms at Earls Court were always overcrowded, a fact that Rose had not even noticed until she went to Chalk Green and learned the pleasures of living in a large and beautiful manor-house.

"I do feel a beast," she said. "And I wouldn't have mum know for the world. But I always want to push the walls out. Oh, Drina, think of Edinburgh!"

Drina did think of it sometimes, with an excited lift of her heart, but before rehearsals started she, her grandparents and Antonia were going touring for a few days.

The trip started by taking the road west, so that Antonia could have a glimpse of the Chilterns and Chalk Green Manor. There was no one at the Manor except a skeleton domestic staff and the gardeners, but Antonia seemed thrilled and, looking round at the deep green woods and the blaze of poppies, scabious and other chalkland flowers, said that it was just as she had imagined England.

While the Chesters remained in the car, Drina led Antonia along the footpaths that led to the top of her beloved Lodge Hill, and there they sat on the wild thyme, yellow stonecrop and wild candytuft, looking round at the Chiltern scene.

"It's beautiful," Antonia said in her own language. "So quiet and still and pale. No brilliant colour, except for the poppies, but lovely in shape. I never imagined anything quite so sunny and hot. I believed that it always rained in England."

Drina thought it must indeed be very strange for her,

in spite of the delightful sunshine, for she remembered the coloured villas of the Riviera, the exotic flowers, the olive groves and the dark blue sea. Camogli . . . dear Camogli . . . with its red and blue and green boats and skyscraper houses. This Chiltern scene was far from the sea and probably there was nothing in the whole of Italy that approximated to it.

They called at the farm to see Jenny – a surprise, though Drina had always hoped secretly that it might be possible – and then spent a night in Stratford, managing by some miracle to get seats for *Julius Caesar*. Antonia was enchanted with the famous English theatre, and perhaps most of all with the gentle, shining river, the drifting swans and the willows growing shadowy in the summer dusk. She insisted, the next morning, on visiting Shakespeare's birthplace and Anne Hathaway's Cottage, and took many coloured photographs to show to her parents and friends when she returned home.

After that they drove through the West Country into Wales, and finally into Cheshire, Lancashire and Yorkshire. One of the highlights of their trip was a night in Wharfedale, and Antonia and Drina climbed Simon's Seat and looked down at the summer beauties of the dale from the rocks, bilberries and heather of the summit.

Then suddenly Drina realized that in three days' time she would be rehearsing at the Dominick Theatre. The ballet season was over and they would be able to use the theatre for rehearsals, which made everything far easier. Now she was looking forward with excitement and uneasiness to what was to come and, though she had enjoyed herself, she was almost glad when they were speeding South. For one thing the weather had changed and they drove through a thick grey mist that was very depressing.

Antonia had her last night at the flat, Ilonka came to supper, and the next morning Antonia was seen off at Victoria.

"You must come to Italy again, Drina," she said, as the time drew near for the boat-train to depart. "Come and see us and then go to your other cousins in Perugia."

"I want to," said Drina. "And I must see my Italian grandmother again. She writes to me every week or two. But I don't know when it will be. Next year, I suppose."

The next morning, shy and excited, Drina and Rose presented themselves at the Dominick Theatre, and then, for nearly a fortnight, life was bounded by the Company and *Casse Noisette*. Everyone was very kind and friendly, particularly Bettina Moore and Terza Lorencz, and young Igor Dominick was often there, sitting in the stalls and eager to accompany Rose and Drina to a café for cold drinks whenever there was an opportunity.

"He's really quite nice," said Rose in astonishment, after the first day or two. "I was scared of him at first."

"He's all right," Drina said casually. "Though he has got such a glowing opinion of himself, I like him." In fact, she counted Igor as a friend.

After the first nervousness Drina adored being Little Clara. The role had always held a special magic for her and there were times when she just could not believe that she was going with the Nutcracker Prince (Peter Bernoise, the principal male dancer) through the Land of Snow to the Kingdom of Sweets. Catherine Colby was dancing the Snow Queen and the Sugar Plum Fairy and she was very charming to the two very junior members of the Company. On one occasion she actually took them out to lunch, and they were at first so shy and overcome that they could hardly speak. But Catherine Colby was a very natural person and she talked so interestingly about her three-year-old daughter and her home in Chelsea that they soon forgot to be shy. In private life she was married to Peter Bernoise and her daughter was called Penelope.

Before they had finished the meal a press photographer suddenly appeared and the photograph was in a London paper the next day. *"Catherine Colby, prima ballerina of the Igor Dominick Company, lunching with two young friends."*

"Mother's going to frame it," said Rose. "Though you'd never really know it was me. My hair looks awful and I seem to have a smut on my nose."

Drina, of course, was far more to the fore than Rose, but the understudy was rehearsed thoroughly, all the same, and Drina was glad that her friend still seemed happy about the arrangement. Rose, in fact, was in seventh heaven at going to the Dominick Theatre every day and knowing that a wonderful week in Edinburgh lay ahead.

The full dress rehearsal was held on the Friday, which gave everyone a chance to travel to Edinburgh on the Saturday, avoiding Sunday trains. Everything went comparatively well, except for one or two of the usual hitches that everyone expects at dress rehearsals.

It was a very chilly day for the end of August and Drina, sitting at the side of the stage throughout the scene in the Land of Snow, for the first time realized what Bettina had meant. It was certainly extremely cold sitting in the draught that came from the wings and it was a relief to get on the throne that was being used for Little Clara during the long act in the Kingdom of Sweets. But she had little difficulty in giving the impression of being amused and delighted by the various characters who danced for her pleasure, and especially loved the Chinese dancers who represented Tea and, of course, the famous dance of the Sugar Plum Fairy. She seemed to know the music with her whole self; she had loved it long before she ever saw the ballet and now had seen *Casse Noisette* danced many times, even learning the Waltz of the Flowers herself.

"I always dread those horrible critics," Drina heard Catherine Colby saying to one of the solo dancers. "They generally seem really savage during the Festival."

"I've never danced there before," said the girl. "I hadn't joined the Dominick last time it went to Edinburgh."

"I've danced there a number of times as a guest artist. It's a beautiful city and the Festival is extremely colourful and interesting, but something always seems to get into the critics."

And Drina registered with amazement that anyone as great as Catherine Colby could still mind what the critics said. It made her own nervous excitement a little more intense, for it was all very well to look forward to being in Edinburgh at Festival time and to be thrilled to have the chance of dancing Little Clara. How terrible if everyone said she was miscast or something. How terrible if one critic said: "*Of course young Drina Adams quite lacks the experience and charming presence needed for Little Clara.*"

She was so restless that evening, and so flushed, that her grandmother felt disquieted and heartily wished that someone else had been chosen to dance Little Clara. She kept Drina busy finishing the last of the packing, then heated her some milk and sent her to bed early.

"It's ridiculous to get so stirred up. And you don't have to dance till Monday evening."

"We have a run-through on Monday morning," Drina remarked.

"Well, forget it now," Mrs Chester said. She kissed Drina's rather hot forehead and left her to read for her usual half-hour before going to sleep.

The next morning they met Rose at the station and took their reserved seats in first-class on the Edinburgh express. On the platform the two girls glimpsed several other members of the Company, including Catherine Colby and Peter Bernoise. Miss Colby wore a pretty pink suit and was drawing a good deal of attention.

"Oh, isn't it thrilling? Isn't it thrilling?" Rose said over and over again. Because she had so few clothes she was wearing her Dominick suit and emerald green blouse. Most of her ordinary dresses and her one coat were decidedly shabby, but, in any case, the uniform suited her very well.

Knowing Rose's predicament, Drina had decided to do the same, though she had a caseful of pretty dresses and had carried her summer coat over her arm. It often made her feel guilty that she had so many clothes, while Rose had so few, and Drina did not as yet greatly care what she wore. Just occasionally she longed to look sophisticated and grown up, but ordinarily she was quite content to wear a plain dress and sandals. That way she felt more free.

Drina and Rose were sitting side by side as the train roared on its way North, and suddenly Drina clutched Rose's arm. Her face was white and startled and her eyes very dark.

"Rose! Oh, Rose!"

Rose, much startled, clutched her in return.

"What on earth's the matter? Are you ill, Drina?"

"Very nearly!" Drina managed to say, after a moment. "Oh, I have been such an utter, utter idiot! All these weeks and I never once thought of it! Oh, I wonder – I wonder – "

"For heaven's sake!" cried Rose, digging her sharply in the ribs. "Tell me!"

"Well, but I never thought – Granny never reminded me! There's been so much to think about, but how *could* I forget? Don't you see? Mr Dominick and Miss Volonaise have never seen me with Granny. And I never gave it a single thought when I heard that they were staying at the Highland, too. And not only that; Granny said she'd be with us in the theatre and I was so glad about your coming with us that I never thought about that, either. There was no one else, and – oh, what on earth shall I do?"

"You mean because of your mother?"

"Of course." Drina was still as white as though something tragic had happened. "I can't *believe* I could be so stupid!" She turned away from Rose and hurried back to her grandparents' seats behind them.

Mrs Chester gave one look at her face and asked resignedly, "What is it, Drina? Do you feel sick?"

Drina plumped herself down on the opposite seat and poured out her sudden realization.

"Granny, they mustn't know. Did you forget, too?"

Mrs Chester said very calmly, "Yes, I did forget. You must believe me, Drina. I was just trying to help you and Rose. Later I remembered but, since there was no one else to accompany you, I decided to say nothing. Besides, we couldn't change our hotel, so I knew we'd have to chance it. Mr Dominick is very unlikely to see me backstage, and as for the hotel – well, they probably think it high time that they met someone closely connected with you. Miss Whiteway took you to the audition and I've just kept away, though I've spoken to Mr Dominick on the telephone a few times. Now stop looking so tragic. It's many years since they saw me and I assure you I've altered a good deal. When Betsy was alive I had red hair. It went grey very quickly after her death."

Drina looked at her, already more calm. She could not imagine her grandmother looking any different. It was a startling thought that she had once had red hair like her daughter and had looked younger and perhaps pretty. Though she was a good-looking woman now.

"They must see a lot of people, of course. But if you knew them well – "

"I dined a few times with the Dominicks, and met both Mr and Mrs Dominick *and* old Igor Dominick at innumerable cocktail parties and parties on the stage. Marianne Volonaise, too, though she wasn't a Director then. As Elizabeth Ivory's mother I naturally came in for some notice, but people are soon forgotten."

"Does it really matter, anyway?" Mr Chester asked.

"Yes," said Drina earnestly. "It matters very, very much to me. I'm sorry if it makes it awkward for Granny, but I *don't* want them to find out that my mother was Ivory."

"They would keep it to themselves," said Mrs Chester quietly. "Now it's time we all had some lunch. Come along, both of you." And Rose, hovering anxiously, stepped back to let Mr Chester lead the way.

The dining-car was already quite crowded when they reached it, but Drina saw Mr Dominick and his son and Marianne Volonaise at the far end. Igor smiled and waved, but Drina and Rose saw no more of him on the journey.

On and on, travelling steadily northwards, and the

excitement of both girls mounted as, at last, they began to pass through the Lowland hills.

"Edinburgh is such a romantic place," Drina said dreamily. "I remember the Old Town – a sort of frieze against the sky in the evening. And the Castle and the Palace of Holyroodhouse. Only Mary Queen of Scots and Prince Charles Edward Stuart didn't mean much to me then."

"But, Drina, I didn't know you'd been! You never said."

"Oh, it was a long time ago. I scarcely remember it. We had a holiday in Wester Ross when I was about nine – yes, it was just before I went to the Elleray School in Willerbury and met Jenny. And on the way home we stayed for a night or two in Edinburgh." It was a holiday that Drina had not thought of for a long time, but now she remembered the shallow green sea that had washed the lovely coast of Wester Ross, the blue islands, the soft Gaelic voices. It had been wonderful, but somehow it had all been quickly swept away by the things that had followed soon after – the new school, Jenny's talk of ballet, her own arrival at the Selswick Dancing School and the deep satisfaction of learning the ballet movements. Nine – nearly ten – and now she was fourteen and there seemed to have been a whole life between.

"We're in Scotland!" said Rose, though she had said it half a dozen times already. "There ought to be bagpipes playing and people in tartan waving to the train."

"There'll be plenty of tartan in Edinburgh, I expect," said Drina. "And bagpipes, too. We've got seats for the Tattoo for our last night – Tuesday week."

Then the city was drawing near and they began to collect their coats and other possessions. The dark cavern of the Waverley Station . . . a taxi procured by a porter . . . then emerging into the dazzling sunlight and Edinburgh all about them. Princes Street ahead and the Old Town behind. Drina twisted round to stare at the half-remembered scene and caught her breath in deepest delight when she saw the old, uneven roofs, the "crown" of St Giles and the great dark bulk of the Castle on its rock.

"Oh, Rose! Rose, look!"

Rose was looking everywhere: at the brilliant gardens; the decorations along Princes Street; at the Castle and the long romantic frieze of the Old Town. Her eyes were not quite dry, for she had seen so little, apart from London, and she was too moved and excited to speak.

The journey was only very short. In two or three minutes they were turning across the long lines of traffic and drawing up before the hotel on the north side of Princes Street, facing the Gardens and the Castle.

"Our rooms are on the front," said Mr Chester, as they went up in the lift, escorted by one of the hall porters. "I'm afraid it will be noisy."

"We shan't mind," Drina assured him. "Shall we, Rose?"

"If it means having that view," said Rose breathlessly, "I don't care if a band plays *The Skye Boat Song* all night long."

Their room was very large, but Rose scarcely looked at it. She rushed over to the window and Drina followed her. They stood side by side, staring down at the bustle of the famous street and then across at that wonderful, sunlit view.

"I think I *must* be dreaming!" cried Rose. "I really think I can't be awake. Oh, Drina, I never knew I could be so happy!"

3
Igor's French Cousin

They had dinner in the hotel's huge dining-room, another new experience for Rose, who was so over-awed by the waiters and the splendour of some of the diners that at first she could hardly eat anything. But by the time the main course arrived her naturally healthy appetite asserted itself and she ate with enjoyment.

The Dominicks and Miss Volonaise were at the far end of the room, Miss Volonaise in a plain but striking black dress, and Drina eyed them with some uneasiness, hoping that it would be possible to escape before they passed on their way to the door. But Mr and Mrs Chester were in no hurry to leave. Mr Chester ordered coffee for all of them and liqueurs for himself and his wife, and Drina saw with a leaping heart that Mr Dominick was rising.

Then he was walking slowly across the room, followed by Igor and Marianne Volonaise. She tried desperately to look the other way, but it was no good. Mr Dominick had seen her and was advancing, smiling.

"There you are, Drina! And Rose!" He was looking expectantly towards the Chesters and there was nothing else for it. Drina, feeling breathless and frightened, introduced them to each other.

Mrs Chester carried off the encounter with calm

assurance, and there was nothing in either Mr Dominick's or Miss Volonaise's face that indicated recognition.

A few pleasant exchanges and the party of three had passed on, though Igor lingered to remark, "Marvellous city, isn't it? We're going to the Tattoo tonight. The late performance."

"We aren't going until a week on Tuesday," Drina got out, and then sank down, feeling as though she had been in acute danger.

Mrs Chester glanced at her white face with some irritation.

"Really, Drina, what a silly girl you are! They didn't remember me."

"No," Drina said shakily. "But I thought they might."

Mrs Chester, if she had had her way, would have sent the girls to bed almost at once, but Mr Chester backed them up when they said that they wanted to go out for a while. So they all walked out into the brilliance of Princes Street. Already it was almost dark, though the sunset light still lingered in the west, and there was floodlighting everywhere. Beds of glowing scarlet flowers leaped into sharp life in the dark Gardens, and the Castle seemed to float on its rock.

They walked through the crowds along Princes Street, hearing strange languages on every hand, and then crossed the road and climbed the Mound towards the Old Town. Distant music sounded on the warm air and Drina and Rose wandered along, lost in enchantment. From the top of the hill they stopped to look back, and both were quite silent at the magic of the scene spread out below them. The glowing lights along Princes Street, the headlights of cars, the dark gardens, with here and there a sharp blaze of colour. The warm breeze brought a scent of grass and carried to their ears the sound of pipe music, presumably from the Castle, where the Tattoo would be taking place.

"It's wonderful! Marvellous!" said Rose at last. "A sort of dream place. Not at all real."

"It's very real," said Mr Chester. "Think of the things that have happened here over the centuries."

"I know," agreed Rose, who, like Drina, had always found Scottish history absorbing. "But just now I can't believe that any of it was real."

They walked up to the Tron Church and then down the Royal Mile towards the Palace of Holyroodhouse, pausing often to look up dark alleys and at an occasional floodlit building.

"Once," said Mr Chester, "one would scarcely have dared to walk down the Canongate at night. It's altered a great deal. I'm glad that some of these beautiful old buildings have been restored. At one time they were slum tenements that were once great houses and I believe you can still see coats of arms over the fireplaces."

They looked through the gates of the Palace to the outer courtyard and the great dreaming building, with the curve of the hill called Arthur's Seat just visible in the pale moonlight. Standing there, Drina could not help remembering Charles Edward Stuart in his brief glory. In that very courtyard, surely, he had sat on his horse and handed out Jacobite favours to the loyalists of the city?

They caught a bus back to the Tron Church and then walked down the hill and returned to their hotel. By then both girls were yawning and willing enough to go to bed, though, as Rose said, it was a great pity to waste any time at all being asleep.

Upstairs in their big bedroom she looked round with pleasure and satisfaction.

"Oh, Drina! Such a lot of lovely space! Even if we

quarrelled we could still keep quite far apart."

"We won't," Drina said lightly. "We never have."

"No, of course not. But I do like to have room to move."

They undressed and bathed and then, by mutual consent, turned off the light, drew back the curtains and stood by the window, looking out at the passing crowds and the glowing Castle.

"I shall never, never forget it," said Rose. "And to think that I might have been in lodgings in some side street!"

Both were asleep within five minutes and the traffic passing below did not disturb them.

"What shall we do this morning?" Rose asked, as they got ready to go down to breakfast.

"I don't know. Grandfather and Granny may want to go to church, but I don't suppose we need. I'd like," said Drina, "to climb Arthur's Seat and look down on Edinburgh."

"Then let's. I'd love to climb something," said Rose, who felt bursting with energy after an excellent night's sleep. From their high window they could just see the graceful curve of the hill beyond the eastern end of the Old Town. "How high is it?"

"Oh, not so high as it looks. About nine hundred feet, I think. But we needn't go up the proper path. We could scramble up the steep part and pretend it's a real mountain."

In the entrance hall they came face to face with young Igor Dominick, who had just come through the swing doors from the street. He looked at them in his usual half-amused way.

"What! Just got up?"

"It's quite early!" Rose said indignantly.

"I suppose so. I got up to go to Mass, and because I was expecting some French relations to arrive."

"After breakfast," said Drina, "we're going to climb Arthur's Seat. Why don't you get out of those very respectable clothes and come with us?"

"Climb?" Igor looked as though he had never used any energy in his life, though he was one of the most virile dancers in the School.

"Yes, *climb*, you lazy boy. But it's not Ben Nevis."

"Oh, I can't. I shall take my French cousin for a walk."

"Is your cousin young?" Drina asked.

"Oh, yes. Fifteen or so. Her name is Marie Larond."

"Then bring her, too. We'd like to meet her."

Igor shrugged.

"Marie doesn't climb. She'd prefer to walk. Thank you all the same."

"Snubbed!" Rose said in a low voice, as Mr and Mrs Chester joined them and they all went into the dining-room.

"Do you think so?" Drina asked doubtfully. "You can never tell with Igor. Even now I can't, when he puts on that manner. Why should he snub us?" She did not expect to be snubbed by people she counted as friends.

A few minutes later Igor passed their table in the company of a very handsome woman and a slim and exceedingly elegant girl. She had chestnut hair and wore a very grown-up pale grey summer suit. On her slender wrists were several bracelets and her pretty, but slightly supercilious mouth was emphasized with vivid scarlet lipstick. Her heels were very high.

"Good heavens!" said Rose, none too quietly. "No *wonder* he didn't think she'd want to climb Arthur's Seat!"

"It's Igor's French cousin," Drina explained, in

answer to her grandmother's enquiring look. "He said she's only fifteen."

"Then she's very unsuitably dressed for a young girl," Mrs Chester said decidedly. "Those heels are positively dangerous. I hate jeans and dirty, uncombed hair, but really there *is* a happy medium."

"All the same, she does look smart," Drina said rather wistfully. There were times when she hated looking so young that people took her for about twelve.

This morning Miss Volonaise and the Dominicks were at a larger table that would also accommodate the French lady and her daughter, and Drina could not help an occasional glance towards it. There was an odd feeling in her heart that she did not remember ever having experienced before. Could it be jealousy? Oh, surely not! But, without thinking about it very much, she had assumed that Igor would be a companion to her in Edinburgh as he had been in Italy, and there he was smiling at the French cousin as though there was no one else in the world.

Drina pushed all thoughts of Igor away and had, in fact, quite forgotten about him as she and Rose set off towards Arthur's Seat.

It was a glorious morning and Edinburgh looked at its most beautiful – the Gardens were bright, the flags of the nations waved gaily in a warm and gentle breeze, and the light slanted across the Old Town, picking out here an ancient house and there a tapering spire.

Neither felt like taking a bus and they walked briskly up the Mound, took a short cut through the old houses into the High Street, which Drina had noticed on her detailed street map, and then set off rapidly down the Royal Mile, finding much in daylight that they had not noticed at night.

"We must go and see John Knox's House," Drina remarked. "But not now. And St Giles, of course. Oh, and the Art Exhibitions, and I believe there's a Photographic Exhibition, too. An international one. I'd like that, wouldn't you?"

"And Holyrood and the Castle," said Rose. "I want to see the Long Gallery or the ballroom, or whatever it is, where they danced while Charles Edward and his army were here. And the Scottish Crown Jewels at the Castle."

"We might do some of it this afternoon," Drina suggested. "We certainly can't tomorrow. We shall be busy all day at the theatre, and then at night – Oh, Rose!"

"I'd sooner you than me," said Rose.

"Would you really?"

"Yes, I would. I'd be scared."

"But you've got to face it some time."

"The *corps de ballet* first, though. You're used to being in front of an audience. I'm not."

They cut across the courtyard of the Palace of Holyroodhouse, where a motley crowd was already wandering about. There were Girl Guides from several different countries, a party of Germans, and what seemed a whole coachload of Americans, all eagerly taking photographs.

Then they crossed the road that encircled the Queen's Park and took to the smooth, grassy slopes of the hill, leaving the stark rocks of the Salisbury Crags on their right. On their other side a little loch was blue as the sky and the cries of sheep filled the sweet, grass-scented air.

It seemed astonishing that only a few minutes before they had been in the Canongate, for this was already like the country. Soon they stopped to look back and saw the velvet lawns spreading about the Palace, with flower-beds glowing brilliantly.

"I'd like to dance on that grass," said Drina. "Oh, Rose, isn't it heaven? Aren't you happy? I can feel happiness just surging through me."

"It's wonderful!" cried Rose. "The most fascinating place I've ever seen."

"But you love London."

"Oh, I do, but so much of it is hideous and, anyway, it's so familiar."

As Drina had suggested, they ignored the broad, gently winding path and set off up a small, grassy valley, where there was no one else at all. The sun was hot and they climbed very slowly, finding the last part of the way very steep. They hauled each other up and then, rejoining the path, climbed the last stretch to the rocky summit, where they stood on the highest point staring all around – at the long coastline of the Firth of Forth, at the hills to the South, and at Edinburgh at their feet, the Castle dwarfed to their left, the long line of the Royal Mile, Calton Hill with its ruins, and the Palace spread out as clearly as a little model on a green carpet.

It was a long time before they decided that it was time to descend and then it was hunger that drove them. They had eaten a good breakfast, but it was already nearly twelve o'clock and they had said they would be back at the hotel before one to meet Mr and Mrs Chester, who were taking them to the Festival Club for lunch. Mr Chester had made them all members and had said that it would be pleasant to use the Club as much as possible.

They were soon down the hill and entering the side gates of the Palace once more, to cut across the courtyard. And there, taking a photograph, was Igor

Dominick, with his French cousin standing a few feet away.

Igor took the photograph and then looked up.

"Oh, hello!" he said casually, and Drina and Rose were both suddenly conscious that they were grubby and untidy.

"Hello," Drina said. "It was wonderful up on Arthur's Seat."

"Such a peculiar name for a hill," said Igor lazily, and introduced them to his cousin.

"How do you do?" said Marie Larond. "You," to Drina, "are the one who is to dance?"

"Little Clara? Yes. Are you interested in the ballet?"

Marie gave a little laugh.

"But yes. I find it charming. Igor and I we used often to go to l'Opéra. But I am not a dancer."

"Marie models clothes," Igor explained proudly.

"I thought only grown-ups did that," Rose said bluntly. She was irritated by the pair of them.

"No, you are wrong. Even small children may be models, and now Marie shows clothes for teenagers. In Paris, you know."

Rose had a sudden impulse to say, "And exactly where did you think we thought she'd modelled? In Texas?" But Drina cut in quickly with a polite, "How interesting!"

"I think we should find Maman, Igor," said Marie prettily, and Igor glanced at his watch.

"Perhaps so. This afternoon we're going to North Berwick." And Igor nodded to Drina and Rose and led his cousin away towards the entrance to the Palace.

Drina was very silent as they walked out through the other gates and up the hill to the bus stop, and Rose, glancing at her face, made no comment. But in the end Drina said, "I think you were right. He doesn't want *us*.

And I was so horribly conscious that we were in our sandals and that I had that green mark on my dress. Look at our hands, too!"

"I don't care," said Rose. "We'd been up the hill and that – that model would never be able to climb twenty feet."

"She's very pretty," said Drina.

"Oh, yes. But she's a silly, affected thing and Igor is affected, too. I thought so from the first, though I got to like him better whilst we were rehearsing."

"In a way he's very grown-up," Drina remarked and then said no more about Igor and his cousin as they made their way back to their hotel.

Mr and Mrs Chester were waiting in the lounge, so the girls flew upstairs to wash, brush their hair and put on different dresses. Then they all four set out to walk to the Festival Club where the building was easily picked out because of the colourful awning, the flags and the flowers in tubs.

A trifle awed, and clutching the membership card that Mr Chester had given her, Rose followed a little behind as they entered the building and passed the uniformed commissionaires. Then, as the glory of the banked flowers in the hall and on the staircase burst on her, she breathed, "Oh, Drina, how beautiful! I've never seen such flowers, never! Those gladioli! Oh, what a lovely, lovely place!"

"It is beautiful," Drina agreed and was glad to think that, for the whole of their time in Edinburgh, they would be able to use the Club.

After lunch they went upstairs and saw more glorious flower displays in the upper hall. Many languages reached them as they moved about and Drina identified in quick succession a French party, some Italians and a party that seemed to be German or

Swiss.

"Oh, it is so interesting! I love this place!" she cried.

"I'm glad you're pleased," said Mr Chester, looking at their eager faces. "And what do you want to do this afternoon?"

"Oh the Castle, please," said Drina. "And if there's time we'd like to look at the theatre. I've found it on the map. It's down by the Surgeons' Hall."

"Very well. But first we'll have some coffee and look at the papers. Don't you want to know what they say about the Festival?"

And Rose and Drina settled down, content to rest for a short time before more excitement.

4

Casse Noisette

The rest of Sunday passed very happily. Both girls were thrilled with the Castle and with the wide views from the battlements, though they did rather wish that the crowds were not so great. But that was inevitable during a hot Sunday in Festival time.

They met Bettina Moore wandering about the Castle by herself, with a camera slung over her shoulder, and she joined them for a time, talking in her natural, easy way.

"A very charming girl," said Mrs Chester, when at last Bettina had gone off to meet another member of the *corps de ballet*. "She's just been telling me that she was alone in England for some years because her parents – her whole family, apparently – were in Australia."

"Yes, but they're back now, I think," Drina said.

"She's very attractive."

"She's very nice!" Drina said warmly. "And she never puts on airs."

"Not like some people we could name," Rose murmured, and Mr Chester asked, amused, "And what do you mean by that?"

"Only Igor and his French cousin. He'll scarcely look at Drina and me because he's got her, and *she* looked at us as though we weren't fit to be spoken to. We met them this morning at Holyrood."

"I'm afraid that Igor isn't a very steady boy," said

Mrs Chester. "Handsome and clever, but he gives the impression of being easily swayed."

They then went to have a look at the outside of the theatre where the Company was to dance, and afterwards sat in Princes Street Gardens watching the passing people. As the day wore on, Drina slipped back into a dream state, a state half of fear and half of acute excitement. Tomorrow . . . tomorrow . . . tomorrow the time in Edinburgh would stop feeling like a holiday and she would be part of the Festival in the truest sense, on a stage facing a big audience.

She awoke very early the next morning and could not go to sleep again, so presently, when she knew that Rose was awake, too, she suggested, "Let's get up and go into the Gardens. I'm curled up with excitement."

She ate so little breakfast that Mrs Chester frowned, as she always did when she knew that Drina was unsettled.

"You may not get time for much lunch. *Do* eat something. I don't want you to be a nervous wreck before the end of the week."

At that Drina laughed. "Oh, Granny, I shan't be. But I can't eat any more. I'll take some biscuits with me."

They arrived at the theatre in time to watch part of *Sea Green Maiden*, the new Dominick ballet, which was being run through first, though it would come last that night. Then, for a long time, there was nothing but *Casse Noisette*. Some of the lighting had to be altered and there was a little trouble over some of the scenery, which did not quite fit the stage, but by the middle of the afternoon they were released, Drina hot, rather tired and more nervous than ever about the evening.

But after a bath and a meal she felt fine again and ready for anything, though little ripples of excitement kept running up her spine.

In the hotel entrance hall she met Marianne Volonaise, who looked at her kindly and asked, "Not nervous, are you? You make a very charming Little Clara and I'm sure all the critics will like you."

"No-o, Madam. It's just that I can't really believe – it's so wonderful to be here with the Company!" Drina said so fervently that Miss Volonaise laughed.

"Perhaps one day you'll come back here as a real member of the Company."

And those few words had the power to send Drina up into seventh heaven, for surely they would not have been spoken if Miss Volonaise had not thought there was a good chance of her going on? The memory of Daphne Daniety came often, and it was clear that there was no safety anywhere. But if Madam said . . . Drina almost literally danced up the stairs to get ready to go to the theatre.

Mrs Chester had ordered a taxi. She sat there looking very composed, and she entered the theatre by the stage-door and walked down the long passages as though it were quite the most natural thing in the world. And, of course, in a way it was, though there had been a gap of many years between.

There were a number of messages and cards for Drina, which pleased her very much. This time she did not have a dressing-room to herself, but shared one with the younger members of the *corps de ballet* who were to be the children at the party. She had scarcely been in the theatre ten minutes before the whole atmosphere of the backstage regions had got into her blood and fear was forgotten in the over-mastering excitement. The smell, the bustle of stagehands and electricians, the knowledge that soon the curtain would go up and the performance begin, made her blood tingle and she really pitied Rose, who was sitting quietly in a corner, watching and listening.

Then Drina was in a frilly pink party frock and pantalettes, with a blue sash round her waist and another ribbon tying back her hair. She was made up and quite ready and the "five minutes" had been called. She stood in the wings looking out at the elegant Victorian drawing-room, with its great window-alcove where the Christmas tree stood. This production was to start directly with the party indoors and not with the guests arriving through the snow.

From behind the curtains came the sound of the overture. It was time to go on stage . . . the ballet was about to begin. And then the magic was real and all about her. It was *her* party, hers and her brother Franz, who was played by the youngest boy in the *corps de ballet*. The guests had arrived – they were all joining in a ceremonial march. Somewhere at the back of her mind as she marched round gaily was an odd little inner picture of what it must look like from the audience. So many times she herself had sat and watched *Casse Noisette*, envying Little Clara, carried away by the bright colours, the whole atmosphere of the party.

"If only Jenny was here," she thought. "I wish she could have seen it."

Then followed the Polonaise by the grown-ups and a wild Galop for the children. Drina's hair danced on her neck and there was no need to act excitement and pleasure. When the tree was lighted and they all gathered round there were tears of sharp excitement in her eyes. This was *it* . . . so lovely! Opening the presents, laughing, displaying them.

Herr Dosselmeyer arrived with his wonderful clockwork toys and everyone waited eagerly while he wound them up and they started to dance. Drina,

sitting on the floor, was for the first time able to glance out into the great dark auditorium. Out there were hundreds and hundreds of people, watching the bright stage.

Herr Dosselmeyer had also brought an old-fashioned wooden doll for Clara. It was carved in the shape of a nutcracker and she was delighted with it. Laughing and eager, she agreed to dance alone, while everyone fell back to watch. Such a short little solo, but important for Drina because it *was* a solo . . . she was most truly dancing with the Dominick.

The act went on. Franz seized the nutcracker doll and refused to give it back to her. The doll was broken and Little Clara was very sad. She rocked it tenderly.

But the party was drawing to an end. After another dance the guests began to leave. Clara helped to put out the lights on the tree. Bedtime . . . the room was empty and Clara paused just long enough to look at the nutcracker doll, propped against a cushion.

There was no interval, and while the footmen made the room ready for the night and drew back the curtains, Drina had to get out of the pink frock and pantalettes and into her nightgown. Then it was time to creep softly back to see if the nutcracker doll was safe.

Moonlight streamed through the window and there was still a faint glow from the tree. The grandfather clock began to strike twelve . . . It was time for the magic to start, for the battle between the toy soldiers and the mice. The nutcracker doll changed into a handsome Prince (Peter Bernoise), wearing white and silver, and he invited Little Clara to go with him to the Kingdom of Sweets.

Sitting at the side of the stage in the Land of Snow, watching the Nutcracker Prince dancing with the Snow

Queen, Drina was so lost and so happy that it really seemed a dream experience. The Snowflakes whirled round her and the curtain came down to a long roar of applause.

Rose was in the wings and she seized Drina eagerly. "You look quite dazed! Did you enjoy it? I was so proud of you, somehow. You looked a lovely Little Clara; just as though you were in a magic world."

Drina blinked and laughed, "Oh, Rose, I was! I suppose, as Bettina said, it might get boring and be cold, sitting there in a nightgown. But just now . . . the rehearsals didn't prepare me for it, somehow. Oh, I loved it!"

"Did you know it's going to be televized?"

They were on their way to the dressing-room and Drina stopped dead, staring at her.

"What? *Casse Noisette*? I knew that *Sea Green Maiden* was."

"It's not going to be now. Something about fitting things in. You know it's a long programme showing bits from several shows and things? The timing has gone wrong and they want to do the Kingdom of Sweets act instead. On Saturday evening."

"Me on television!" And then Drina added delightedly, "So Jenny will be able to see! Oh, I'm so glad! Oh, Rose, how exciting! But how terrifying, too. Not just hundreds of people but millions! It'll be live, not recorded. Say something goes wrong?"

"Nothing will, you idiot. Why should it?"

On the stage the stagehands worked rapidly and when Drina stood again in the wings with Peter Bernoise the icing-sugar palace was in place, with its steps and pillars. The curtain rose and Drina and the Prince were greeted by the Sugar Plum Fairy in her crisp pink tutu. Very soon Clara, smiling and eager, was led to her throne and there was nothing to do but to watch the *grand divertissement* and to clap and smile.

First the Spanish dancers, then the *Danse Arabe* and the amusing Chinese dance, Trepak and the Dance of the Mirlitons. Easy to smile and look happy and thrilled, because that was exactly how Drina felt. It was for her, Little Clara, and for Drina Adams, too. Just a few performances as part of the whole, part of the Dominick Company. And the Dominick Company was dancing for *her*. Small wonder that a hardened critic wrote next day:

"Drina Adams as Little Clara gave us a feeling of real enchantment. She looked as though it was all new, all wonderful. I am sure that many eyes kept straying to her on her little throne, a small, nightgowned figure facing fairyland."

The Waltz of the Flowers and the *grand pas de deux*. And afterwards the Dance of the Sugar Plum Fairy seemed more brilliantly and delicately performed. Then the last ensemble, with all the brilliant colours whirling about the stage, and Little Clara, holding her nightgown, leaping up to dance, too, as the curtain came down.

The applause was tremendous as the curtain rose again and again. Then Peter Bernoise and Catherine Colby went several times through the curtains to the front of the stage. Suddenly Catherine Colby held out her hand and said, "Come on, Drina!" and Drina was there between the two great ones, curtsying and smiling, convinced that none of it was real. How *could* she be standing there between two great dancers, smiling at the unending applause?

She was dazed and silent as she took off her make-up and put on her ordinary clothes, and Mrs Chester was only anxious to get her back to the hotel.

"But I want to watch *Sea Green Maiden!*" Drina protested.

"Well, you can't tonight. You've had a hard day. Is Rose ready? Then come along, the pair of you. Your grandfather said he'd leave during the interval and find a taxi for us."

The taxi was there and Mr Chester hauled Drina in.

"You were splendid. I enjoyed it all, and I don't mind in the least missing that very modern new ballet. We knew you'd be tired tonight."

"I'm not tired," Drina said, still in a slightly dazed voice. "Oh, Grandfather, I did love it so! And I'm starvingly hungry!"

He laughed.

"We'll order sandwiches and milk – "

"Couldn't we go to the Festival Club? I shall never sleep if I do go to bed."

"Not tonight," Mrs Chester said, very decidedly, and was much relieved when, the milk and sandwiches finished, Drina and Rose went up to bed.

"Was it really good, James? I watched from the wings, but you can't get a proper idea."

"It seemed to me very good and Drina looked as though she had been on the stage for years. So much assurance and so much spontaneous happiness. Then when she took that curtain with Peter Bernoise and Catherine Colby – "

"Well?" his wife asked, noting the change in his expression.

"Well, she didn't look a day more than ten in that nightgown, but – she was very like Betsy. The same rather wide smile. She has Betsy's mouth, if not her colouring. It seemed as though the years – "

"I know," she agreed with a faint sigh. "I keep on remembering Betsy. I still wish that we could have achieved a different life for Drina."

"It was no good. The child *has* to dance. I think there'll surely come a day when she dances the Sugar Plum Fairy."

"Yes, I'm afraid so," said Mrs Chester. "It's what she wants, but it will take her far away. I find myself dreading it."

5
Drina's Unlucky Day

Drina and Rose both slept late, but the Dominick party and Marianne Volonaise had evidently done the same, for they were all in the hall, and just about to go into the dining-room, when Drina and Rose appeared. There were congratulations for Drina from everyone, even from Marie, who had evidently been in the audience with Igor. But there was a slight bite in her remarks, all the same.

"So charming!" she said. "Such a child you looked. It is most amazing when you have fifteen years."

"Fourteen," Drina said coolly, meeting the smiling hazel eyes with more assurance than she had felt on Sunday. The fact of Igor's withdrawal still hurt, but she would certainly not let him guess that she minded his absorption in his French cousin.

She was thrilled that Mr Dominick and Miss Volonaise seemed pleased with her.

"Have you seen the papers?" Mr Dominick asked.

"No, not yet. We – we didn't wake up – "

He laughed.

"We had them sent up to our rooms and generally the critics have a kind word for you, though one says the dancing as a whole wasn't up to standard, and another, feeling savage, says we'd be better if we worked."

Drina went very pink.

"Oh, the beast! The Company's marvellous this year – "

Miss Volonaise laughed rather ruefully.

"It's never easy to take, but others do praise us highly, especially for the new ballet. I shouldn't worry."

Drina ran off then to ask if there were any letters and there were several for her: one from Jenny, one from Ilonka, and cards from Meryl, Bella and Jan. She looked at them while they were waiting to be served and of course opened Jenny's letter first.

"Dear Drina, (Jenny wrote)

"Here I am back home and really wishing I were still at the farm. Two of the boys are away, but Donny and Bill are here and I plan to take them out, though heaven knows where to. There's precious little to do in Willerbury, as you know. Philip will be home this week until he goes back to London.

"Things are still upsetting here. Sometimes I wonder what will happen. Father looks worried and Mother does too, and I'm sure her hair is greyer every week. What if I have to leave school and get a job? Sometimes I wake up in the night, just shaking and thinking it has really happened. But it's no use looking for trouble. Only it would mean that an agricultural college was impossible, I suppose, and possibly no farming.

"Anyway, don't let me worry you, when you must be having a wonderful time in Edinburgh. I hope you have a great success. I will be thinking about you all the time.

"I'd love to see Edinburgh. I'm like Rose and haven't really been anywhere. But I can imagine it all decorated, and the sun shining (how lucky the weather is so good!), and the Castle and everything.

"Oh, by the way, before I left the farm I saw Robert Hogden again. We were invited there for the evening, and I was dead right. He had a girlfriend staying there who fitted quite well with my description. Gipsy Jenny, eh? She was fair and

rather fluffy and lisped. *Her name wasn't Maisie, but Molly, so I wasn't far out, even over that. But I don't think they are engaged or anything.*

"Dance your best – I know you always do – and have a good time and send me lots of postcards.

"Love from,
        Jenny."

After breakfast Drina chose a colour photograph of the view from the Castle and wrote to Jenny:

"Last night was wonderful and I took two curtains with Peter Bernoise and Catherine Colby. Casse N. is being televized on Sat. evening, so you can see it. I'm so glad. Do hope everything will be all right. Love, Drina."

Tuesday was an entirely free day and they drove out into the Pentland Hills (Mr Chester having hired a car) with a picnic lunch, which they ate by a brown stream in the heart of the hills. Then, late in the afternoon, they all went to see the Palace of Holyroodhouse and Drina stood for some time in the long room where the Jacobite supporters and the Clan Chiefs had danced, though she thought that Charles Edward had not often joined in. In her mind's eye she could see him standing against the dark panelling, splendid in Royal Stuart tartan and wearing his decorations – a handsome, almost fairy-tale Prince, whatever historians said about his later life.

Rose was especially fascinated with the oldest rooms and little dark staircases and said her blood ran cold when she thought of the murder of Rizzio.

That evening they went to a foreign film, which the girls enjoyed, though perhaps Mr and Mrs Chester did not, and altogether it was a pleasant, sunlit day, packed with interest.

"Then tomorrow the matinée!" said Drina, as they stood at their window with the light out, watching the brilliant scene outside. Though it was their fourth night in Edinburgh it still enraptured them. "In the end everything comes back to dancing, doesn't it?"

And Rose, yawning, agreed.

The matinée went off well and Drina enjoyed it, though it had not quite the deep thrill of Monday evening. Afterwards, as they ate a rather late tea at the hotel, Rose said to Mrs Chester:

"I do hope you don't mind, but I thought perhaps it would be best. Bettina asked me if I'd like to go out with her and some of the other members of the *corps de ballet* tomorrow. She was going to ask Drina, too, but I said you were all going to Dunfermline to see Mr Chester's business friend."

"You were very welcome to come with us," said Mrs Chester. "But it might have been dull for you. Drina really *must* come, as the Crawfords have never met her and expressed a special wish to do so. Where are you going?"

"To the coast, I think. To somewhere called Tantallon Castle. I didn't think you'd mind."

Drina had agreed with Rose that she would have more fun going out with Bettina. She felt a little envious, but knew that she must do her duty and accompany her grandparents. After all, her grandmother was being very unselfish in accompanying them to the theatre and, anyway, it would be exciting to see the Forth Bridge.

Mr Chester had again arranged to hire a car for the day, as the Crawfords lived in the hills, some miles beyond Dunfermline.

"But we must be back in plenty of time," Drina said anxiously. "I'm dancing in the evening."

Her grandfather laughed. "We're only going for lunch. It isn't really so very far. Don't worry, my dear."

Rose went off soon after ten, and Mr Chester collected the car and brought it to the hotel. Drina sat in the back with her hair blowing in the breeze from the open window, and it was pleasant to speed away from the city – even though she loved it so much – into the country to the north. The corn had been cut and the pale stubble fields gleamed in the sun. The sky was very blue, with dazzlingly white clouds, and when, suddenly, they reached Queensferry and saw the vast structure of the Forth Railway Bridge, she caught her breath in wonder and delight.

"Why, it's beautiful! So huge against the sky! Oh, I'm sorry that Rose is missing it."

"But she'll enjoy being on the cliffs near Tantallon," said her grandfather.

The sparkling blue water and the great bridge continued to thrill Drina and, when they stopped in the ancient city of Dunfermline for a time, she was equally thrilled with the warm golden-grey stone, rather like that of the Cotswolds, and with the great Norman nave of the Abbey. Then they went on northwards, presently taking a climbing secondary road and then, after consulting the map, an even more narrow and lonely one.

"The Crawfords have borrowed this house for a month from some friends," Mr Chester said, indicating a low stone house on the far side of a little loch.

"Too lonely for me," Mrs Chester remarked. "Though the countryside looks very pleasant on a day like this."

They received a very warm welcome and Drina was regarded almost with awe by Mrs Crawford, a rather colourless-looking middle-aged woman with a breathless voice.

"So this is the little ballet dancer? And the actress, too, aren't you, dear? We saw you in *Dear Brutus*. Such a charming play, I always think, and that poor child left in the wood. . . ." She talked on and on, not waiting for replies, while Mr Chester and Mr Crawford – who was a quiet man with a slight Scottish accent – talked business at the other side of the room.

The house was attractive, with a pleasant garden, and the lunch was excellent, but Drina was soon rather bored and restless. Looking out at the hills and the sparkling loch she longed to be able to run away and be free in the sun, but obviously that would be rather rude and her grandmother would certainly not approve. So she continued to sit on the little terrace, listening to the conversation of the grown-ups.

Presently the men wandered off to look at something in a distant part of the garden and Mrs Crawford insisted on showing Drina and her grandmother all over the house, talking without ceasing as they moved from room to room. Mrs Chester made an occasional murmured reply, but Drina had even stopped listening. She wandered after them, her hands clasped behind her back and restlessness rising in her like a wave. It was already three o'clock. Surely, surely they would be leaving soon? Of course it probably wouldn't take long to get back, but they were some miles north of Dunfermline.

"Still four hours before I have to be at the theatre," she told herself sternly. "Don't fuss, you silly girl."

Mrs Chester looked at her own watch and said that they must soon be leaving, and Mrs Crawford stopped a monologue about decorating to say, "Oh, but it's quite early! You'll be back in Edinburgh in no time."

At half-past three they were downstairs again and the men had come in from the garden. Mr Chester also looked at his watch and said that they must be going, and Mrs Crawford immediately made for the kitchen, saying over her shoulder, "Just a cup of tea before you leave. I always like a cup about now."

"No, really – " Mr Chester began firmly, but she had already gone and Drina gave him an agonized glance.

He smiled at her to tell her not to worry, that there was plenty of time, and after ten minutes or so the tea came.

In the end it was nearly half-past four before they managed to get themselves out to the car, and by then Drina was tense and cross, more with boredom than anything else. She did not think they were really likely to be late.

But the hired car refused to start and her heart gave a wild and sickening leap.

"Oh, Granny!"

Mrs Chester, seeing her white face and tense body, put her hand on her arm and said quietly, "Don't worry."

Eventually the car did start and Drina leaped into the back. Never, as they went down the short drive and away past the little loch, had she been so glad to get away from anywhere. Mrs Crawford's endless talking and the feeling that they would never, never be able to leave had worked her up to a great pitch of nervous tension.

"I never knew a woman to talk more," said Mrs Chester, with a sigh. "I really thought we'd never get away."

"And Crawford is so different," Mr Chester remarked. "Such a steady, quiet chap. A typical Scot, I always think. She must be a great trial to him."

"Probably ceased to take any notice of her long ago," said Mrs Chester, with slight asperity. Self-contained and controlled herself, she had much disliked the almost hysterical chatter, though naturally she had had to be polite.

The car travelled all right for about four miles and then the engine began to splutter. Drina's hands clutched the seat and her knuckles were white.

"Oh, please, no!" she almost prayed. But the car was stopping and her grandfather, looking concerned, got out to peer into the engine.

"It really is too bad," he said, in a muffled voice. "I wanted the car we had on Tuesday, but this was said to be in perfect running order. I can't *see* anything wrong, but then I've never been much good at repairs."

"But what shall we *do*?" Drina asked frantically after five minutes, when the car was still stationary and not even a cyclist had passed them on the secondary road.

"Calm yourself, Drina," Mrs Chester said repressively, but she, too, looked anxious. Years of living with Betsy had forced deep into her mind the knowledge that one must never be late for a performance.

"I can't! It'll soon be five o'clock. Oh, if only someone would *come*!"

But the only people who passed them were two girl hikers going in the opposite direction, and in the end Mr Chester said, "I think there was an AA box where we turned off the main road. It'll only be a mile and a half to two miles now. I think I'd better walk on, and perhaps a car will come along and give me a lift."

"Oh, let me come, too!" Drina begged. "I can't stay here doing nothing. It will be better to be moving."

So they left Mrs Chester in the car and set off at a rapid pace. A few cars passed them going in the

opposite direction, but they were little more than half a mile from the main road by the time they got a lift. As luck would have it an AA man passed them and he gave them a lift back to the car. By then it was all a nightmare to Drina, and she sat on the bank while the AA man tinkered with the engine, her eyes aching in the bright sunlight, not even attempting to listen to the technical jargon that the man flung at Mr Chester. Engines meant less than nothing to her, except that she expected them to behave well and take her where she wanted to go.

Now that she was back by the car she thought that she had been very silly not to ask to be allowed to thumb a lift to Edinburgh, but Mr Chester would never have agreed to her going on alone with strangers.

Drina sat on the hot grass and watched the minute hand of her watch move rapidly on. This was worse – a thousand, thousand times worse! – than that winter day when she had been lost in the snowy woods with Petrouchka when she should have been on her way to London to dance at the Dominick matinée. It would have been bad enough to miss the students' show, but this was a real performance at the great Edinburgh International Festival. Drina pictured Rose waiting frantically at the hotel and wondered how on earth she could get a message to her. Rose would have to go on ahead and be ready to dance.

Perhaps, in her secret heart, she would be glad, but that was not the point. The point was that the girl who should have been dancing, the girl the Company had chosen and was paying to dance, was sitting on a bank somewhere in the wilds of Fifeshire, quite helpless to do anything.

In the end it was well after six before the car gave a hopeful whirr. The AA man, who now knew all about the desperate need to be back in Edinburgh by seven, gave a shout of triumph.

"There now, lassie! In you get. She'll go now."

And go "she" did, with slight protest at first. The man promised to telephone the Highland Hotel and send a message to Miss Rose Conway as soon as he got back to his post, and the Chesters and Drina drove off, Drina by then so lost in the nightmare that she sat with her eyes closed, not even opening them as they went through Dunfermline and took the road to North Queensferry.

"I wouldn't have had this happen for the world," said Mr Chester, who was deeply distressed.

There was a long queue to get on to the bridge. Drina gave a frantic moan and Mrs Chester did not even tell her to be quiet. Now the sparkling Firth of Forth and the great railway bridge meant nothing to Drina. She was already ahead in spirit, seeing Rose setting off for the theatre, knowing quite certainly that they were going to be too late.

When at last they were on the bridge she willed the car to hurry with all her might, her eyes huge in her white face. Oh, how quickly the hands of her watch were moving! Oh, why couldn't time be held back somehow . . . somehow?

"I'm afraid we won't do it," said Mr Chester, as they drove slowly through the traffic at Queensferry. "Oh, Drina, I'm so very sorry."

"You couldn't help it," Drina murmured. She was still lost in the nightmare, still somehow hoping that a miracle would happen.

But it was certainly not Drina's lucky day. There was another hold-up near Dean Bridge. There had been an accident between a coach and an estate car and the road was temporarily blocked.

In the end they crawled past the scene and went slowly through the Edinburgh traffic. It was twenty-five to eight as they reached and crossed the High Street. Drina had said she would go straight to the theatre, as her shoes and everything were there. But she knew that it was too late. By the time they reached the theatre the first act would be under way and Rose would be dancing.

6

The Understudy

Drina burst in at the stage door, white and unhappy, only wanting to make it clear that it was not her fault, that she wouldn't for the world have let the Company down. And there, in the passage that led to her dressing-room, was Mr Dominick.

Drina flung herself at him, all awe forgotten, frantically pouring out the sorry story of delay and accident.

He let her talk, knowing that it would mean some relief to tension. Then he said quietly, "It was unfortunate, but these things will happen. Sometimes they happen more often than we like, but you couldn't help it and you've been upset enough. Calm down, my dear. It won't make the slightest difference to our regard for you, and you'll be dancing again on Saturday – twice."

"But Rose – was she very upset? Has she gone on?"

"Yes, she's dancing now." Mr Dominick at last looked at Mrs Chester, who had remained, quite silent, a little distance away. She came forward then.

"It was all most unfortunate. My husband and I are very much upset."

"A chapter of accidents!" Igor Dominick said lightly. Then he put his hand on Drina's thin shoulder. "Look! I'll write you a note so the people at the front of the house will let you stand at the back of the Circle. Don't you want to watch Rose?"

Drina gave a little gasp and then looked up at him.

"Oh, yes, please! It would be better than the wings. Oh, I'd never have done it on purpose, but now – I'm glad that Rose is having her chance. I – I've felt rather bad about her."

He looked at the pale, eager face, no longer so tense, and merely smiled. But he added one more good mark to the girl whom he had somehow been unable to ignore since the day she arrived at the Dominick School. Many of the junior students were little more than names to him, but Drina Adams had personality.

The note was scribbled and Mrs Chester said quietly that she would sit in the dressing-room and wait for Rose. Drina slipped out past the stage door man and round to the front of the theatre. Showing her note, she was allowed to go upstairs, and she went into the ladies' room to wash her face and comb her hair. Her dress, luckily, was a crisp red one that did not crease or show the dirt. Assuring herself with a hasty glance in the mirror that she didn't look too disreputable to grace the Circle, she slid forward like a little ghost, the music telling her before she had properly focused the stage just what point the ballet had reached.

The party was almost over and Little Clara was saying good-bye to the guests, then helping her parents to put out the lights on the tree.

Drina drew in her breath sharply. Rose looked so pretty in the pink party frock with the frills and the blue sash and, by the time the stage was dark and Little Clara was creeping back in her nightgown, the dreadful events of the afternoon were fading and Drina was relaxing into the odd dream state that she sometimes brought to ballet.

It ought to have been her . . . but it wasn't. It was

Rose. And so Drina leaned there, behind the curving rows of seats, still glad in the depths of her heart that out of the fright and the unhappiness had come one good thing. Rose, for one evening, anyway, was not sitting in a corner of the dressing-room, unimportant and often ignored.

In the interval Drina bought herself an ice and then followed it with coffee, since she was very hungry. Then the curtain rose again on the Kingdom of Sweets and Rose arrived with the Nutcracker Prince, smiling and starry-eyed. She would know now that Drina had arrived and was watching, so perhaps she could enjoy herself thoroughly. Certainly she looked happy and not in the least nervous. Now she was on the throne, watching the first part of the *grand divertissement*.

The watcher at the back of the Circle followed every movement of the ballet until the final ensemble and the swift descent of the curtain, and she joined in the applause as warmly as anyone there, clapping until her hands hurt. Curtain after curtain for the whole Company, then the Nutcracker Prince and the Sugar Plum Fairy alone. Now Rose . . . and there she was between them, smiling and curtsying. For one moment of almost savage envy Drina wished that she was there, in her rightful place, but the feeling passed as the curtain rose again on the final gathering of the whole Company.

And Drina was not denied at least one small triumph. She was standing there, wondering whether she could possibly stay to watch *Sea Green Maiden* and thinking perhaps better not, when a schoolgirl of about twelve said clearly:

"But, Mummy, I'm *sure* it's Drina Adams! I'd know her anywhere after Monday night. It was such a terrible disappointment to find this other girl, but here she is –

the real one. Couldn't I – couldn't I ask her to sign my programme?"

"It *can't* be her, dear," said the well-dressed woman in a low voice. "You know they announced that owing to unforeseen circumstances – "

"Perhaps she hurt her foot or something." The schoolgirl was staring at Drina with such utter admiration and wistfulness that Drina stepped forward shyly. It was an odd feeling, for, always leaving the theatre before the end of a play or ballet, she had met few fans. If they had waited at the stage door she had not seen them.

"I *am* Drina Adams and of course I'll sign it, but I haven't a pen."

The schoolgirl looked helplessly at the little evening bag she carried and her mother produced a pencil.

"This is the best I can do. Are you really the girl who should have danced?"

Drina found herself giving a hasty sketch of the day's happenings.

"I got here after the ballet had started, so Mr Dominick let me come and watch Rose."

"She was good," said the schoolgirl, clutching the signed programme as though it were very precious. "But you – I *had* to come again. Isn't it the most wonderful thing in the world to be Little Clara?"

"Yes," Drina said simply.

"I know I am being very cheeky, but how old are you?"

"Older than I look. Fourteen," said Drina and, seeing her grandmother making her way towards her through the crowd, smiled and escaped.

Mrs Chester said briskly, "Rose is all right and I told her you were watching. She's changing now and then she's coming to watch *Sea Green Maiden* with you. I'll wait behind. I'm sure you're both dead tired, but you can sleep late in the morning."

Just before the house lights went out Rose arrived breathlessly at Drina's side, and the schoolgirl, hearing their voices, looked eagerly round from her seat three rows in front.

"Oh, Drina! It was all so awful! I felt so terrible about you. But then I got onstage and forgot to be nervous, and in the interval your grandmother said – she was very nice." She was very flushed and still starry-eyed.

"I got here to watch just as the party ended," Drina whispered and, as the lights went down, they stood at the back of the Circle, ready to watch the very modern movements of the strange new ballet, *Sea Green Maiden*.

By the time they were travelling by taxi through the lighted streets both were so tired that they could only yawn and blink, but part of Drina's mind was given over to the recurring magic of Edinburgh. The floodlit buildings seemed to rock a little and, as they stopped in a brief traffic jam in Princes Street, the sound of pipe music came to them on the breeze.

"O-oh!" Drina said, yawning again. "I'm so hungry! Then I think I'll sleep for twelve hours. And on Saturday I'm going to sit on the doorstep of the theatre all morning just to make sure! I shall never, never forget this afternoon if I live to be a hundred!"

7

Ivory's Daughter

It was wet on Friday but, to Drina and Rose, Edinburgh still looked romantic in the rain, and that night they went to see the Dominick's other programme, *Les Patineurs* and *Giselle*. They had seen both ballets many times, danced by a number of different companies, but such was their mood that they enjoyed every moment. Drina in particular lost herself so completely in *Giselle* that it was half an hour later before she came back to the real world.

"I wonder, shall *we* ever dance Giselle?" she said to Rose, as they sat over sandwiches and milk in the lounge of the Highland Hotel. "Can you imagine it?"

"I can just about imagine being the most unimportant wili," said Rose with a sigh. But she, too, while the ballet lasted, had had dreams of one day holding a great audience with the perfection of her dancing.

When they arrived at the theatre for the Saturday matinée the television men had already been there and there were wires and cameras in unexpected places. But it was the evening performance, the last act of *Casse Noisette*, that was being televized, and the afternoon performance seemed a curiously lighthearted affair. There were a great many children in the audience and they cheered in a most uninhibited way when Drina took her curtain with Peter Bernoise and

Catherine Colby.

Mrs Chester insisted that she should rest on her bed for half an hour between performances, before having an early meal and, though Drina protested fiercely that she was not in the least tired, she had to obey. Rose sat on the edge of the bed, reading out bits about the Festival from the newspapers, and the time passed very quickly.

"To think that it's the very last time!" Drina said with deep regret, as they went back to the theatre by taxi. "But we still have a few days of the Festival left. The play on Monday and the Tattoo on Tuesday. It won't be quite an anti-climax."

There was an especially excited air about the theatre, though the television cameras were not yet on. Drina found herself savouring every moment, even the sheer pleasure of being in a dressing-room, dressing and getting made up. Once she looked at her little cat mascot, Hansl, and thought of her mother, whose own mascot it had once been. Hansl had stood now on dressing-tables in the Dominick Theatre, the Queen Elizabeth Theatre, and – most surprising of all – in the Opera House, Genoa. Drina never went anywhere without her mascot and would scarcely have dared to dance without the knowledge that the little cat was there.

So the ballet started for the last time, the guests arrived and the tree was lit up. Beyond the footlights the huge audience sat in complete silence, as lost, perhaps, in the magic of the scene as Little Clara herself, moving so gaily about the stage in her pink frock and pantalettes.

When the interval came Drina was literally ablaze with excitement and her grandmother saw it with characteristic misgiving. But there was no nervous element in it, Drina was merely utterly carried away by the enjoyment of the occasion, by the astonishing knowledge that in a very short time the ballet would be seen by people in distant places. Perhaps they would be sitting in remote farmhouses in the hills, in the Chilterns and the Cotswolds and Wales. In London, too, and of course in Willerbury. Her last thought as she stood in the wings with the Nutcracker Prince was that, in Willerbury, Jenny and perhaps her mother would be waiting in the familiar sitting-room – waiting to watch *Casse Noisette* on an Edinburgh stage, hundreds of miles away.

And so Little Clara and the Nutcracker Prince stepped out into the blaze of light to meet the Sugar Plum Fairy, and simultaneously the cameras and sound apparatus went into action, so that every note of music and every expression on the faces of the dancers was carried to all those places that Drina had thought of, and many more.

Far away in London Ilonka and her mother, and the new little kitten called Binki, sat in the sitting-room above "The Golden Zither" restaurant, waiting to see Terza in the Waltz of the Flowers and Drina as Little Clara. Mr Lorencz would have liked to see them, too, but Saturday evening was a busy time and he could not leave the restaurant. In fact, Mrs Lorencz felt guilty at being upstairs, when there was work to be done, but Ilonka had persuaded her. So they watched the screen and were presently told that they were seeing an Edinburgh theatre, where the last act of the ballet *Casse Noisette* was about to begin. And then there was Drina, small and wide-eyed in her nightgown, holding the hand of the Nutcracker Prince as she stared about the wonderful Kingdom of Sweets.

Ilonka clutched Binki so tightly that the small furry

body quivered and the kitten gave a small wail of protest. But Ilonka never even noticed, though her hands did relax automatically. She was carried away by the wonder of seeing her friend on the television screen.

And in Willerbury, Jenny sat on the floor, silent and tense, while her mother knitted in the background, curious to see Drina Adams dancing with a real company.

As the screen flickered into life and Drina and the Nutcracker Prince stepped out on to the stage, Jenny gasped and clasped her hands very tightly. She was not an imaginative girl, except where her feelings were most closely touched, and in this case they were very deeply moved indeed. For Jenny really regarded Drina as almost a sister and it was to her a most extraordinary experience to sit in her home and watch that ghost of Drina, smiling and enchanted, being led across a distant stage to sit on a little throne.

Throughout the ballet Jenny neither moved nor spoke; she seemed scarcely to breathe. Again and again the cameras picked up Little Clara on her throne, catching the alert, delighted expression on the little face below the soft, shining dark hair.

The music that filled the room was very familiar to Jenny, though she was no great ballet fan. At last it was the final ensemble, with the little girl in the nightgown jumping up to mingle with the dancers.

Then down came the curtain in that far Edinburgh theatre and the applause filled the Willerbury room. It rose again to show the assembled company, then fell and rose again and yet again. The voice of the commentator said:

"And that is the end of our Edinburgh Festival programme. But we will just wait to see the principals.

Ah, yes, here they come!" And there was Drina before the curtain with Peter Bernoise and Catherine Colby and bouquets were being handed up to both Little Clara and the Sugar Plum Fairy. For just a moment the cameras held the ballerina and then Drina, wide-eyed and smiling, and that was the end. The screen went dark and Mrs Pilgrim came forward to turn off the set.

Jenny looked away hastily, but not before her mother had seen her face.

"Why, Jenny!" she cried in utter astonishment, for she had never before seen her daughter cry because she was moved by music or a book. "Why, Jenny!"

"I can't help it!" Jenny sobbed, groping for a handkerchief. "It's so idiotic, I know, but it was so strange and she looked so – so like herself and yet so unlike. I can't believe that we ever – that we're friends. I can't believe that we'll stay together. She'll go far away."

"She may become great and famous," said Mrs Pilgrim. "But you can be sure that she won't forget you. Why, Drina feels that you're a sort of rock in her life."

"She'd better!" said Jenny and, much ashamed at her exhibition of feeling, bolted into her own room, where she cried for some time, partly because she had been very much moved and partly because she had been secretly miserable for a considerable time. Things were still worrying in the Pilgrim household and her future seemed in some doubt.

"Oh, Drina, I wish you were here for one of our long talks!" she mumbled into the coverlet, as she knelt by the bed. And then, characteristically, she sniffed back her tears, leaped to her feet and went to wash her face. After that she was her usual calm self.

On Sunday morning Drina left Rose writing postcards and set off alone towards the Gardens. She did very much need time to sort out her thoughts and it was a fine morning again, though cooler.

On the pavement just outside the hotel she ran full tilt into young Igor Dominick, who was alone. He grinned just as though he had not ignored her for a week.

"Hullo, Drina! Where are you off to in such a hurry? Would you like me to come with you?"

Drina had stopped dead, and now she looked up into the handsome, assured face.

"You're quite a stranger. Where's Marie?"

"She has gone," Igor said, shrugging. "They travelled overnight to London."

"You must certainly miss her," said Drina, coolly. She could not resist the jibe, for the hurt caused by Igor's total desertion was still there and was immediately aggravated by his calm conviction that she would now be glad of his company. Perhaps it was wrong to be proud, but she would never feel the same about Igor again. They might return to friendly terms, but she would never trust him to behave as a real friend.

"Oh, yes," Igor said casually. "She is very charming, Marie."

"Well, I'm sorry, but I'm busy now." And Drina nodded and strode briskly across the street during a lull in the traffic.

She was still walking very fast close to the flags of the nations when she came suddenly face to face with Igor's father.

"Good morning, Drina," he said, for they had not met in the dining-room. "How do you feel now that it's all over?"

"Oh, I'm sorry it's over," Drina said earnestly. "It was wonderful. I'll never forget it."

"You did very well. Have you seen the papers this morning? One or two more nice things are said about you." He gave her a very thoughtful look and then said with extreme deliberation, "Has it ever occurred to you that if the critics knew you were Elizabeth Ivory's daughter you would get infinitely more notice taken of your every stage appearance?"

Drina was so much astonished and so utterly dismayed that she went quite white and stared at him with her mouth open. She couldn't speak and he put his hand on her arm and drew her to a seat.

"It's not very warm, but we'll sit here. I've been wanting a word with you. It is true, isn't it? You *are* Ivory's daughter?"

Drina merely nodded, her hands tightly clasped, and he said gently, "Why didn't you tell us? Why has it been a secret for so long?"

Drina had got her breath, but her heart was still hammering. She said faintly, "I – I wanted to succeed, if possible, on my own. I thought – if people knew – I told Mr Amberdown that – "

"Amberdown? Does *he* know?"

"Yes. It was he – he told me. I mean he thought I knew. It was at Covent Garden just before – just before I came to the Dominick."

It was Mr Dominick's turn to look astonished.

"You mean to say you didn't know yourself? Not until then? When was it? Two or three years ago? Look here, my dear, I think you'd better tell me the whole story."

And Drina told it, at first stumblingly, then with more assurance as she almost forgot his presence. She told about always wanting to dance and her grandmother's obvious disapproval, her desire that Drina should not have anything to do with ballet. She told about Jenny and the Selswick School, but explained that Miss Selswick had had no idea of her identity, though then she had sometimes used her real name of Andrina Adamo; of the move to London and her solitary practising until she met Miss Whiteway by chance in a bookshop in Victoria Street. And then she most vividly described that night at the Royal Opera House, when, under the blazing lights, she learned her mother's name and that she had been perhaps the greatest dancer of all time. Then something about her deep determination to keep the whole thing a secret, to fight on alone.

Watching her pale face, with the black hair swinging forward occasionally, Igor Dominick saw the pieces of the puzzle fitting together, and the early respect he had felt for the child deepened and grew. Elizabeth's girl . . . the baby who had almost literally been snatched away by Elizabeth's mother after the accident that had cost the dancer her life. The child, it had been freely said, who would never be allowed to dance. And the child had won, perhaps a little in the way that red-haired Betsy had won. Igor Dominick, though he had only been a young dancer himself then, well remembered glimpses of Betsy in the School, remembered her first appearance on the stage and how her personality had gradually broken through shyness and an initial awkwardness that had seemed likely to stop her being much of a dancer. He saw, in his mind, pictures of Betsy . . . Betsy Chester turning into Elizabeth Ivory, great and acclaimed. He saw her most vividly on that night when she had danced Josette in *The Breton Wedding*. Less than twelve hours later she was dead and the world mourned someone who might have gone on to unimaginable heights.

Sitting on the seat with Betsy's daughter, with the

Princes Street traffic roaring in the distance, the Director of the Dominick Company thanked heaven for this pale child's determination to be a dancer. She had beaten her grandmother, beaten circumstances, and, as plain Drina Adams, had made a good start already. Whether she would be in any way great remained to be seen, but –

He put out his hand and took Drina's cold one.

"It was very brave and determined of you to want it to be a secret and, if you wish, it shall remain so. Only Marianne and I know, you know. We haven't mentioned it to anyone else."

Marianne! If Drina had been less occupied she would have noticed and felt that she had been admitted to a sort of intimacy with Igor Dominick.

"I – I don't want people to know. But, in any case, it's all spoilt. I wanted to get there myself – if at all."

"My dear girl," he said, amused, "you have got where you are entirely alone, and I solemnly promise you that we won't be influenced by the fact that your mother was Ivory."

"But how did you guess? Was it Granny? I was so afraid that you might recognize her. I told her – I made her promise – "

"Well, actually you have reminded us of someone for a long time. We often puzzled about it. But, yes, it was your grandmother. I didn't recognize her immediately, but later I began to wonder, and Marianne wondered, too. We both remembered meeting Elizabeth's mother on a number of occasions and, though she has altered – well, anyway, Marianne sent to London a week ago for her collection of photographs and we found there were several groups at parties in which Mrs Chester figured. We even found a photograph of *you*. A mere baby, but the eyes and hair were the same. Does Rose know?"

"Yes, now," Drina admitted. "But not for some time. We went to the film of *The Breton Wedding* together when it was revived and it was such – such a strange experience that I had to tell her."

It must indeed have been a strange experience, he thought, seeing your mother for the first time as a shadow on a cinema screen.

"Rose thinks I'm mad," Drina confessed. "She says she'd have told, especially when Queenie – " She stopped abruptly, blushing.

He laughed. "You mean because her mother was Beryl Bertram and she sets such store by it?"

"Yes-s".

"Another thing occurs to me. Who were you staying with in Milan in the spring? Whom did Igor go out with? That time you took him to Stresa and Isola Bella."

"My Italian grandmother. I'd never seen her before. Granny – this Granny – hadn't wanted me to meet her till then."

"Good heavens! Andrina Adamo! And I never knew. So you swore her to secrecy, too?"

"She wanted to ask you for cocktails or a meal," Drina told him. "I don't think she really understood, but she was very good about it."

He rose abruptly.

"It's getting chilly and you don't want to catch cold. I suppose I may talk to your grandmother now? I wanted to ask you first, since I supposed it was you who were keen on the secret."

"Oh, yes," Drina said, suddenly very shy. "She's in the hotel lounge, reading the papers."

Igor Dominick walked purposefully through the Gardens and across the road. He was looking forward with a strange mixture of feelings to talking to the woman who had brought up Ivory's daughter.

On Tuesday evening Drina and Rose sat with the Chesters in seats on the Castle Esplanade, watching the Military Tattoo. The Dominick Company had gone back to London and in the morning they themselves would travel South. Meanwhile Drina was quite lost in the superb spectacle that had been moving before her for the past hour or two. It was quite dark, but the lights blazed all around and the romantic bulk of the Castle made a backcloth that rivalled any she had ever seen in a theatre. It had been a hot day, with a heavy shower in the early evening, and the slight drifting mist added to the strangeness and beauty of the spectacle.

But now it was nearly over . . . the marching, the Highland dancing, the colourful foreign troops. The lights had gone out, including the floodlighting on the Castle, and then one bright beam picked out a solitary piper high on the battlements.

Drina's spine prickled with excitement and appreciation. Oh, it was wonderful! Such marvellous staging!

She would be deeply sorry to leave Edinburgh, especially before the Festival ended. But she would come back.

The pipe music died away, and, after a pause, the lights sprang up again. People began to move rather stiffly and Drina drew a long breath.

"I shall never forget any of it."

"Come along," said Mrs Chester briskly. "It's time to go."

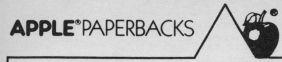

APPLE®PAPERBACKS

More books you'll love, filled with mystery, adventure, friendship, and fun!

NEW APPLE TITLES

☐ 40284-6 **Christina's Ghost** Betty Ren Wright   **$2.50**

☐ 41839-4 **A Ghost in the Window** Betty Ren Wright   **$2.50**

☐ 41794-0 **Katie and Those Boys** Martha Tolles   **$2.50**

☐ 40565-9 **Secret Agents Four** Donald J. Sobol   **$2.50**

☐ 40554-3 **Sixth Grade Sleepover** Eve Bunting   **$2.50**

☐ 40419-9 **When the Dolls Woke** Marjorie Filley Stover   **$2.50**

BEST SELLING APPLE TITLES

☐ 41042-3 **The Dollhouse Murders** Betty Ren Wright   **$2.50**

☐ 42319-3 **The Friendship Pact** Susan Beth Pfeffer   **$2.75**

☐ 40755-4 **Ghosts Beneath Our Feet** Betty Ren Wright   **$2.50**

☐ 40605-1 **Help! I'm a Prisoner in the Library** Eth Clifford   **$2.50**

☐ 40724-4 **Katie's Baby-sitting Job** Martha Tolles   **$2.50**

☐ 40494-6 **The Little Gymnast** Sheila Haigh   **$2.50**

☐ 40283-8 **Me and Katie (The Pest)** Ann M. Martin   **$2.50**

☐ 42316-9 **Nothing's Fair in Fifth Grade** Barthe DeClements   **$2.75**

☐ 40607-8 **Secrets in the Attic** Carol Beach York   **$2.50**

☐ 40180-7 **Sixth Grade Can Really Kill You** Barthe DeClements **$2.50**

☐ 41118-7 **Tough-luck Karen** Johanna Hurwitz   **$2.50**

☐ 42326-6 **Veronica the Show-off** Nancy K. Robinson   **$2.75**

☐ 42374-6 **Who's Reading Darci's Diary?** Martha Tolles   **$2.75**

Available wherever you buy books...or use the coupon below.

Pack your bags for fun and adventure with

SLEEPOVER FRIENDS™
by Susan Saunders

Join Kate, Lauren, Stephanie and Patti at their great sleepover parties every weekend. Truth or Dare, scary movies, late-night boy talk—it's all part of **Sleepover Friends!**